Death at the Midnight Dragonfly

Susan Boles

Death at the Midnight Dragonfly
Copyright © 2017 Susan Boles
Print ISBN: 978-0-9979093-5-7

First Print Publication: November 2017
Cover design by L.L. Pix Designs
All cover art and logo copyright © 2017 by Argent
Ocean Publishing.

A Lily Gayle Lambert Mystery

An Argent Ocean Publishing book
Copyright 2017 by Susan Boles

Death of a Wolfman

"...a charming southern cozy chocked full of engaging characters, laugh out loud humor, and inviting small town charm." Kathi Daley, Author of the Zoe Donovan Cozy Mysteries

"...fast-paced and funny. A true Southern mystery with a flavor as authentic as sweet tea." Jenna Bennett, Author of the Savannah Martin mysteries.

Cherry Cake and a Cadaver

Ms. Boles has a good sense of mystery, and using clues to lead the reader down the right path to guessing the outcome, if the reader is paying close attention. ~Lisa Ks Book Reviews

Ms. Boles is a master baker of cozy mysteries. The multiple story elements are mixed together just right and make Cherry Cake and a Cadaver a worthy addition to the series and a tasty read in its own right.~Back Porchervations

Lily Gayle Lambert Mysteries

Death of a Wolfman

Cherry Cake and a Cadaver

Death at the Midnight Dragonfly

Also by Susan Boles

Fated Love

Sins of the Mother

Acknowledgements

Special thanks to Jeannie Daniel, LuAnn Summers and Kelly Braun for their winning idea entries in the online party to create recipes for Harley Ann's food truck business which begins as a side story in this book. The recipes can be found at the end of this book. And also Special Thanks to Julie Fetter for coming up with the winning name for the food truck itself. I appreciate y'all more than I can say. I love writing these books and I love hearing from fans of the books. A huge Thank You to all the readers who have found the Lily Gayle Lambert mystery series, read the books and loved them enough to let me know. I could not do this without all of you.

Many Thanks also to all the friends and family members who support me in my endeavors. I can never express to all of you how much that support means to me.

CHAPTER ONE

Elvis Presley's voice singing *Winter Wonderland* greeted me as I opened the door to the Grits and Gravy Café to meet the girls for our regular Thursday morning breakfast get-together. We don't get much snow in Mississippi, but we sure do love Elvis.

I glanced around, taking in the garland looped along the walls and the big Christmas tree decorated to the hilt standing next to the cash register counter, noting that the Grits and Gravy was again sponsoring some Angel Tree kids.

Me and the girls had already adopted our angels off the tree and bought the gifts. That'd been a fun trip to locally owned shops so we could support small businesses in addition to making Christmas special for some kids. Next to Dolly

Parton's Imagination Library, Angel Tree is my favorite group to help make children's lives special.

Miss Edna, Harley Ann, Missy and Dixie sat around our regular table smack in the middle of the room. I walked over to them while nodding to Helen in answer to her silent question about did I want chocolate gravy for breakfast. Being as how I always ordered it, Helen was just going through the motions with the questioning look at me.

Maybe someday I'll shock the socks off her and order something different. Nah. I love my chocolate gravy fix too much to give up my once a week treat.

"Good morning, Ladies." I greeted everyone as I pulled the last empty chair and sat down.

"Bout time." Miss Edna grumbled. "We were fixin to start without you."

"We most certainly were not, Miss Edna." Dixie said, frowning at the older woman. "Lily Gayle is only a minute late."

As we waited for our food to arrive, Miss Edna said. "When I get home I'm gonna mix up my special punch for the Christmas party tonight. I want to make sure there's a gracious plenty for everybody." She shook her head sadly. "Last year we ran out before the party was half over."

Dixie and I looked at each other with raised eyebrows. Using the mental telepathy that belongs to lifelong friends, I knew we were both wondering where Miss Edna got her supply of her secret ingredient.

In all these years we'd never figured that one out. And we'd actually staked out her house a few times over the years trying to catch the delivery.

Heck, maybe she brewed it up in her shed out back. Nothing would surprise me about Miss Edna. She's a product of the generation that made do, made it themselves or did without. Maybe it was also the secret ingredient to her prizing winning dahlias.

Wouldn't *that* be a hoot?

Every man, woman and child in town knew the secret ingredient was moonshine, but kept quiet about it 'cause Miss Edna was so darn proud of her special punch. Right about then I noticed that the folks at the next table over had gone quiet. Listening to our discussion no doubt.

Hmph. Nosy bodies.

Out of the corner of my eye I caught sight of Patsy Hammond. The wife of the local bank manager and as stuck up and pretentious a hussy as you'd meet in a month of Sundays. She never had time to talk to anybody and her husband hovered over her so much it'd bout make a body sick.

But she sure was quick to stick her nose in where it didn't belong so she could spread everything she heard. I was actually a bit surprised to see her without her husband. They were usually like Siamese twins.

"That's so sweet, Aunt Edna." Said Harley Ann, snapping me out of my dark thoughts. "How cool that you have a special punch that you bring to the Christmas party. And that everybody likes it so much."

Everybody at our table pressed their lips together tight, trying to hide smiles at her sweet naivety. This would be her first Christmas in Mercy and she came across as being pretty giddy about the whole thing.

I was right on the edge of a mental eye roll when I remembered she'd spent a lot of the past Christmas holidays in a prison cell after being tricked into driving a getaway car by her previous boyfriend. She'd come to Mercy to start a new life and I should be more supportive of her.

I gave myself a mental kick in the ass for being such a snobby bitch. Lord help. If I didn't watch out I'd end up just like Patsy Hammond. And speaking of the Devil, I cut my eyes over and noticed her ears all but flapping in her effort to hear what we were talking about.

She reminded me of some of the mean sorority girls from my days at Ole Miss. Not *my* sorority, of course.

Dixie kicked me under the table and I gave her a hard look. *What the heck?* "So, Missy." She said. "Tell us all about the latest happenings from the real estate world."

Missy beamed, pleased as punch. She loved dishing with us over the news she gathered from being the only real estate agent in the whole county. Of course, there wasn't a lot of real estate activity in Mercy, but Missy could usually entertain us with stories she heard from all over the county and sometimes the surrounding ones. Leaving out the names of the parties involved, if it was a delicate subject.

It didn't take a genius to figure out who she was talking about most of the time. But it kept her in the clear as far as telling people's personal business.

"Well." Missy paused, then went on. "Did y'all know the new boxing gym up in Olive Branch opened up? I heard people from all over are heading over there to join."

All of us exchanged looks and Miss Edna pushed her chair out from the table in preparation for leaving.

"Wait." Missy motioned Miss Edna to pull back up to the table. "I was saving the best one for last."

"Well, get on with it, girl." Huffed Miss Edna. "I'm not getting any younger sittin' here and I need to get my punch mixed up so it can get good and blended before the party."

Missy blushed to the tips of her ears, but the rest of us just ignored the remark. Classic Miss Edna and we let it roll on off. Avoiding looking at Miss Edna, Missy pulled herself back together.

"There's a sleep study going on up at the Midnight Dragonfly." She paused for effect.

A cone of silence descended over the table. I wasn't sure if we were all on the same wave length, but *my* first thought was that the Midnight Dragonfly, formerly known as Mitchell Manor, was the last place anyone should be opening some kind of sleep study. The place had a bad record for murders happening and I know I'd have a hard time gettin' a wink of sleep in that place.

But how the heck had I missed this nugget of information?

"Yes!" Missy continued. "It's the most excitin' thing to happen around here in a long time." She lowered her voice and leaned in to speak quietly. "Just between us, I was sure that dang old big mansion was going to sit there empty forever. Especially after that business with Luxen getting killed up there. *And* that whole mess with the Mitchells before that."

Missy took a sip of her coffee and went on. "The doctor who's running the study got funding for it from the state. Can you imagine? And he put an ad in the paper a couple of weeks ago looking for local people to sign up to be part of the study. He said he especially wanted more than one generation of a family to participate if they would."

"Why in tarnation would he want that?" Miss Edna asked irritably. "And a fine example of our tax dollars at work. Why would anyone need a to study how a whole family sleeps, I ask you?"

Missy pouted. Obviously disappointed that she hadn't gotten a bigger reaction from us.

"I don't take the newspaper," I said, "so I guess that's how come I didn't know about the sleep study going on." I grinned at them all. "But don't tell Marlene and Alvin that I don't subscribe."

Miss Edna snorted. "Likely they already know that, as small at that paper is."

Just as I was getting my dander up, Dixie interrupted.

"Simmer down, y'all. I want to hear more about this sleep study even if y'all don't care." She patted Missy's arm. "You go right on with what you were saying, Missy."

"So, the biggest part of the story is that the doctor conducting the study said he lived up at the Mitchell place when he was a kid." She buttered a biscuit with deft strokes. "But I don't remember him living here at all." She bit into the biscuit, chewed and swallowed. "I don't know why he'd make up something like that though. Besides. His name is Vlad Templeton and it's not like that's a name anyone would forget hearing."

I caught Dixie looking at me with raised eyebrows.

"I can't imagine more than one person being named Vlad Templeton," I said. "So it's probably him."

"Him, who?" Harley Ann asked.

"When we were all kids, there was a boy our age who lived up at the Mitchell place." I patted Harley Ann on the hand and added as an aside to her since she was pretty new in town herself. "It's the Midnight Dragonfly now, hon." And continued. "His parents worked there. Seems like his mama was the cook and I'm not sure what his daddy did. Vlad was sick with something. Maybe diabetic. I remember he had to take shots regularly and always had sugar cubes in his pockets. You wouldn't remember him, Missy because he was home schooled."

CHAPTER TWO

Bah Humbug. I thought to myself as I stood in the chilly December air of downtown Mercy later that evening. Across the parking lot, in the old train depot building, party-goers dressed in their Christmas best gathered in groups beyond the un-curtained windows.

Folks must have already been into the Christmas punch based on the animated conversations that appeared to be going on inside. Big smiles. Arms waving.

Oops! I saw a splash of red punch swish over the side of a cup being waved around and splash onto Marlene from the newspaper. *That* would be hard to get out of the cream colored sweater sporting a big red reindeer head. Marlene screamed, jumped back and slammed into someone

I couldn't see from my angle. She looked to be apologizing pretty hard to whoever it was. Probably more punch had been spilled onto someone's holiday wear.

I sighed, wishing I felt more animated about attending the Mistletoe Magic Extravaganza, as the annual Mercy Christmas Party was called.

But I just didn't seem to be in the Christmas spirit. I'd had a bit of it when all of us girls had done our Christmas shopping for the Angel Tree kids. But it's seemed to fizz out after that.

I'd had a very busy time with dressmaking. Coming up on the holidays is one of the most lucrative time of the year for my custom dressmaking business. Everything from Renaissance to Old South for women belonging to various historical groups wanting new dresses for their historically accurate Christmas celebrations.

Maybe that had made my personal Christmas cheer go out the window because I seemed to be over the whole merry and bright thing even though Christmas wouldn't be here for two more weeks.

Why, I hadn't even put up my Christmas tree or stockings. And forget about any seasonal display on my big front porch. A shocking state of affairs according to my best friend, Dixie.

She'd been over to the house just yesterday complaining about my lack of enthusiasm. I'd poo-poo'd her words, but deep down, I knew she was right.

And now, here I was, lurking outside the annual town Christmas party in a decidedly non-merry state of mind. The party's pretty much a command performance though. I kicked the tire of a truck in frustration.

The only effect *that* had was to scuff the toe of my brand new leather boots. And that just deepened my bad mood.

I sighed. Maybe a cup, or two, of Miss Edna's special recipe Christmas punch might set me up right for the party. Good thing this was an adults only party and those who didn't care for alcohol in the punch brought their own drinks. Funny how traditions come about in small towns.

However, Miss Edna came with Miss Edna's punch. And ever since she'd worked with Dixie and me a few weeks ago to help solve the mystery of who killed Luxen Natolovich up at the Midnight Dragonfly Inn, and who killed the wolf man before that, she bout near drove me crazy wondering when our next 'case' would come along.

Personally I thought she was grieving over the death of her old flame recently. And how everything had come out about Luxen's life that prevented him from asking her to marry him all those years ago.

I considered myself lucky that she hadn't brought any of that stuff up again at the breakfast this morning. She'd sure enough been in a mood.

Guess she got distracted by the information about Vlad and his sleep study.

Oh, *Lordy*. Would Vlad be here at the party? I sure as shootin' didn't want my first meeting with him after all these years to be in full view of most of the town.

I looked through the big window again at the swirling crowd but didn't see anybody I don't already know. Maybe Vlad didn't know about the party.

I was considering turning around and heading on back home when an odd hissing sound caught my attention. I scanned the area for the source and there, at the side of the building, I saw Dixie with Jack.

From the expression on her face and the way she was waving her arms around, it looked like she was upset about something. And, as usual, Jack stood listening without protest to whatever his wife had gotten her panties into a twist over.

Just as I was about to head on over and mediate, Christmas music and laughter spilled out into the frosty night as someone exited the building through the front door of the depot. Turning my head I spotted Miss Edna. *Yikes.*

I quietly slipped into the darkness, half squatted between two trucks and watched to see if she happened to be leaving the party. Not my classiest moment.

She scanned the area, took note of Dixie and Jack, shook her head, then, walker thumping along, made her way down the sidewalk in the direction of her house. The depot door slammed open and a young woman in a short dress and tall boots called, "Aunt Edna! Wait!" Then hurried down the sidewalk to Miss Edna's side.

Harley Ann.

I watched until I thought they were far enough away they wouldn't turn around and see me, then rose from my partial squat. My thighs screamed in protest. I hadn't done anything close to a squat in a long time.

You'd think with all the walking and bicycle riding I do it wouldn't be an issue. Must be a different group of muscles or something.

As I shifted my weight around trying to eliminate the cramping muscles, my foot caught in a divot on the ground and I stumbled into the side of a truck. I caught myself with a hand to the bed and glanced over the side.

A jumble of junk littered the bottom, half covered by an old tarp. I didn't recognize the banged up old truck, so I took a closer look. An unfamiliar vehicle parked outside the Christmas party was a rare event.

A glance into the interior of the truck revealed a lot of shadows. A bright red pair of boxing gloves spilling out of a gym bag caught my attention. I couldn't think of anyone I knew who was doing any kind of boxing.

Missy had mentioned the gym at breakfast but not anyone she knew who was going there. Still at a loss for who the truck belonged to, I took a couple of steps to test my ankle. It twanged a bit, but took my full weight. No excuse there.

Looking around for another excuse to duck out, I saw Dixie and Jack were still in a heated discussion at the side of the building, so I moseyed on over in their direction to see how I could help.

"I cannot believe you went to Tom Hammond and asked for a loan," wailed Dixie as I walked up behind her. Jack glanced at me, and Dixie turned.

"Oh, hey Lily Gayle." She grimaced. "You just walked into a hornet's nest."

"Now, Dixie" Jack said. "Don't make it out to be more than it is." He shook his head, rolling his eyes. "It's not a big deal."

"Not a big deal?" Dixie fisted her hands, and, thinking she might throw a punch at Jack, I stepped aside so as to be way out of the line of fire. Dixie wasn't known for her accuracy when throwing punches and I didn't want to become a victim of circumstance if she let fly with her fist. "You have embarrassed me to death going to the bank for a loan. Why, once Tom Hammond spreads the word, I'll be mortified."

"I don't think he can say anything about bank business," I interjected. But when Dixie cut her eyes at me, I decided to just step on back some more. My boot heel caught on something and I looked to see what it was. I didn't want fall backward on the asphalt. Before I could make out what it was, Dixie went on with her rant.

"What town do you think you're living in, Lily Gayle? You know how it is around here. Everyone will know before tomorrow is out."

At that auspicious moment, the door to the depot banged open again and the man under discussion pushed past Dixie and Jack, staggered to the side of the building and barfed into the bushes right in front of me.

As the three of us stood in dumfounded silence, Tom Hammond staggered off toward the town square. Jack moved to follow, but was stopped by Dixie's hand on his arm.

"Where do you think you're going?" she asked in an ominous voice.

"I'm going to make sure he's okay."

"No. You're not." If looks could kill, Jack would be dead on the ground from the sheer poison in Dixie's eyes. I'd seen her mad a slew of times. And I knew Jack had, too. But both of us stood rooted in place tonight. The woman standing before us was one neither of us knew.

Jack put his arm around his wife's shoulders and murmured. "Dixie. Honey. This isn't like you. I'm sorry as I can be to have put you in such a state."

After a tense moment, Dixie relaxed her head against Jack's shoulder. He looked at me and said. "Reckon we'll be heading on home now, Lily Gayle."

I nodded and watched as they walked across the town square toward their old Taurus, haloed in light as they passed under streetlights and more shadows once they passed beyond the lights.

Jack made no move to help Tom Hammond who was puking some more in the bushes along the square. I said a little prayer for Dixie as Jack helped her into the passenger side of the car. I knew she'd feel awful about making a scene as soon as she got herself back to normal.

I glanced back through the windows at the laughing partiers and decided I couldn't walk in there and participate. I considered going in just long enough to find Ben and let him know about poor old Tom, but decided no harm could come to him in this town and so went on home myself.

CHAPTER THREE

After I'd had my breakfast the next morning, I debated taking the bull by the horns and running up to the Midnight Dragonfly to see with my own eyes if Vlad Templeton was actually my old friend or, by some incredible coincidence, a total stranger with the same name.

But first, I pedaled over to the It'll Grow Back to check up on Dixie. I came down the sidewalk to the shop, leaned my bike against wall and peered around the edge of the big plate glass window into the shop. Dixie was there alright. Arranging hair products on a stand where she kept them for sale.

She didn't look like she was still in crazy mode, so I took a chance, eased the door open. Dixie jumped like a scared cat when the bell chimed. When she saw it was me tears filled her eyes the same time her cheeks flamed red. Rushing over, she hugged me so hard I thought she might just crack a rib or two.

"Lily Gayle! Thank goodness you came by. I'm so distracted I don't know what to *do*."

I patted her back gently while I tried to loosen her death grip. What could have gotten in to her? It's not like I'd never seen her have a fight with Jack in all these years. I finally managed to break free long enough to go back over to the door and lock it.

Something was seriously wrong here and I didn't want any customers walking in on Dixie in such a state.

Once the door was secured, I led Dixie to the back of the shop where she had a tiny office and sat her in the swivel chair. In the fluorescent lighting, surrounded by boxes of hair products and shelves of paperwork, she looked worse than she had last night.

"Now. Tell me what in tarnation has gotten into you."

"Oh, Lord, Lily Gayle. Me and Jack had the awfullest dust up you ever saw last night."

I laughed. "Yeah. I was there for part of it. Remember?"

With a trembling hand she pushed her hair back from her face. "No. I mean after we got home. I lit into him so bad about going to the bank for that loan that he slammed out of the house and stayed gone all night."

I sank down on a stack of boxes at chair height to take *that* in. I had never known of Jack to get so mad he stormed out of the house. And for him to have stayed gone all night was really out of character. My heart hurt for Dixie.

I reached over and took her hand in mine. Waited till she looked up at me. "Now, hon. I understand you're beside yourself. But you know Jack will be on back home soon."

Dixie sniffled and rubbed the back of her other hand under her nose like a child. "He's never, ever, done anything like this. What if something happened to him? I tried to call him on his cell phone but he doesn't have it with him. I found it on the floor in the living room when it started ringing."

I silently cursed Jack to hell for staying gone this long. I didn't think anything bad had happened to him 'cause Ben would have gotten word by now if that was the case and would've moved heaven and earth to get to Dixie and make sure she heard it from him.

I stood up. "You know what? You come on up to the Midnight Dragonfly with me. That'll take your mind off things still Jack brings his sorry ass back home."

Startled eyes met mine. "What? Why are you goin' up *there*?"

At least I'd gotten her mind off Jack for a minute. "I want to go up there and see if it's Vlad from when we were kids."

She tilted her head. "Of course it's him, Lily Gayle. How many Vlad Templeton's could there be in the world?"

I brushed some dust off my shirt that must have been on the edge of the shelving in here. Dixie kept the shop itself sparkling clean, but wasn't much on keeping it so spotless back here where no one else ever came.

"I reckon you're right. And I'd just as soon have my first meeting with him after all this time be private." I nudged her foot with mine. "You should come. He was your friend, too."

She gave me a sly smile. "As I recall, you had a big ol' crush on him back then."

Her statement caught me off guard and heat rushed into my cheeks.

Dixie gave a delighted laugh. "You're *blushing*."

"I am not. That space heater you've got under your desk has it so hot in here a body can hardly breathe."

Dixie scooted away from the built in desk and pointed to the space heater. Which was off.

"Well." I said. "It must be a hot flash then."

Dixie laughed again. "You haven't been havin' hot flashes before. I think maybe you still have a soft spot for him."

"Don't be ridiculous." I huffed, getting mad now. "You're making a big deal out of nothing."

"If you say so." She shuffled some papers on her desk around. "But methinks the lady doth protesteth too much."

I stood up from the boxes, brushing more dust off my shirt. "Oh stuff that Shakespeare crap. Are you coming with me or not?"

Dixie stood, too. "Nope. I have someone new coming in for a color treatment and I don't want to cancel on a new customer." She hugged me, then stepped back. "But thanks for coming by and cheering me up. You're right. Jack will be on home soon. He's probably up at that gym in Olive Branch working out his frustrations with his witchy wife. I forgot to mention the other day at breakfast that Jack joined it."

I left Dixie getting her station ready for the new customer, but in a much better mind set than the one I'd found her in. That made me happy. But riding my bike in the cold wind out to the Midnight Dragonfly sure did put a damper on my enthusiasm for the trip.

As pedaled my bike up the curved driveway to the house, I saw Ben's cruiser parked out front and he stood on the steps observing the scene. In the driveway, the county rescue ambulance idled with lights strobing red beacons across the scene. Two EMT's worked frantically on someone lying on the big front porch as a third hustled over with a gurney.

As two of the EMT's lifted a tall body onto the stretcher, I stood up and pushed hard on the pedals to quicken my pace to the house. As I got close, I saw the person lying still as death on the white sheet and my heart stopped. Then galloped to catch up.

Tom Hammond.

I glanced around, looking for a clue as to how the bank manager had ended up here on the porch of the Midnight Dragonfly when I'd last seen him in the town square. Gazing around curiously, I noticed a pair of bright red boxing gloves under a bush by the stairs. *What the heck?*

My memory flashed back to the truck I hadn't recognized last night in the parking lot on the town square -- and a pair of boxing gloves spilling out of a gym bag. I wondered if they were the same gloves.

Then I remembered Dixie telling me just this morning about Jack joining that boxing gym.

But, the boxing gym *was* new and I couldn't be sure of who might have joined. And besides, there could be a perfectly reasonable explanation for why a pair of boxing gloves were lying on the ground like that.

But my intuition told me that they were related to Tom Hammond being on that gurney in the back of an ambulance that was now hauling ass down the long drive toward the road back to town.

As I turned back to the porch I saw Ben frown at me over the shoulder of a man who's back was toward me. Then, with a resigned look on his face, he motioned to me to climb up the steps. When the man Ben'd been talking to turned, I realized with a start that it must be Vlad. All grown up and handsome as the devil.

CHAPTER FOUR

The news had traveled with the speed of light through town by the next morning. Or at least the speed of technology. Not being an expert on these things I can believe they're about the same. At least in a small town. Those old-school party lines have been upgraded to smart phones to catch up with the twenty-first century.

I reckon everyone in town must have bout near rubbed their fingerprints off with all texting and calling that must have taken place. Tom Hammond was dead. And it looked like he'd been murdered. He wasn't well liked, but who would actually kill him?

I rushed right on over to the It'll Grow Back beauty shop to consult with Dixie. And to fill her in on Vlad. And to make some sneaky inquiries about Jack's boxing gloves. I didn't want to scare the pants off her, but I *did* want to know if Jack's gloves were at home.

Not that I thought for a minute that he'd done anything to Tom. I just wanted to go through the motions and cross him off the list for sure.

As I came down the sidewalk in front of the shop I looked in the big picture windows and saw every chair in the waiting area had somebody in it. And, just like the other times, my blood boiled just a little bit on Dixie's behalf.

I'd bet dollars to donuts not more than one or two of them actually had an appointment today. They were showing up as walk-ins to get the latest gossip.

You'd think if they had the sense God gave a goose they'd go on and switch over to the It'll Grow Back as their regular beauty shop. They certainly seemed to be spending a good bit of time in it as 'walk-ins' just to listen in on all the juicy gossip that'd happened around here in recent history.

I spotted Mildred in Dixie's chair and I knew her regular wash and set was on Wednesday afternoon. But at least she was a regular customer.

As I pushed open the door, the bell jingled and Dixie looked up. When she saw it was me, and knowing me well, she cut her eyes to the crowded waiting area and gave me a no-nonsense *keep your mouth shut* look. I nodded to let her know I got the message.

All the women squished into the waiting area up front looked up at me, then back down at their magazines like some kind of freaky synchronized act. I halfway expected them all to suddenly turn a magazine page in unison.

"Well. Looky who's here. Lily Gayle will have all the news straight from law enforcement headquarters." Mildred cackled as she caught sight of me. "Come on over here by me so I can be sure I hear all of it."

Before I could make a move in any direction, the Stepford wives up front all looked up again. This time with a glint of interest in their eyes. I shuddered inside.

Acting like I didn't even see them, I made my way back to Dixie's chair. *Not* to fill Mildred in on anything. But so I could get a feel for when Dixie might be done and could step outside with me to chat.

Before I got three steps into the room, Glen Miller music blasted out of my cell phone. I must have accidentally turned up the volume when I slipped it in my pocket earlier. Mildred cackled again and shook a crooked finger at me.

"I bet that's Edna's ringtone. I know she loves that swing music."

I ignored Mildred as I thumbed the phone to silent. Whatever Miss Edna wanted would have to wait a gosh darn minute.

Dixie put the last roller in Mildred's thin white hair and assisted her over to a dryer, lowered the hood and clicked the timer on. It'd take half an hour or so for Mildred's hair to dry so Dixie should be able to slip out back with me for a minute to discuss the latest news.

And so I could sneak in some questions about Jack.

A chilly wind skittered down the alley behind the beauty shop. And the low clouds made the atmosphere even more gloomy. I huddled against the wall as Dixie pulled the sleeves of her cardigan down over her hands.

"Why are we back here skulking around like a couple of criminals instead of sitting in my nice warm office?" Dixie asked.

"Because I want to make sure we're not overheard." I shivered a bit wishing I'd brought my heavier coat. It's one thing to stay warm riding a bicycle while wearing a light weight jacket and a whole other matter to stay warm in that lightweight jacket while standing around in a windy alley.

"Oh, mercy! Please tell me you are *not* on another secret squirrel mission." Dixie moaned.

"Hey! You've solved both of those cases with me. And now you're calling it 'secret squirrel'"?

Dixie blew out a breath, frosting the air around us. "You *dragged* me into helping you with those cases. Please. Let's not get involved in this one. My nerves can't take any more."

I looked both ways in the alley, even though I knew no one else would be fool enough to be standing out here on a cold December morning. But, somehow, it seemed like the smart thing to do. Even though I didn't see anyone, I leaned close to Dixie and spoke low.

"There was a pair of boxing gloves up under the bushes at the crime scene."

Dixie went absolutely still. Not a breath stirred her upper body as her skin turned the color of marble. Then, a loose strand of hair ticked against her face in the wind, breaking the trance. Reaching up to capture it, she whispered.

"I'm scared, Lily Gayle." Tears sprang into her eyes. "When I heard the news this morning, all I could think about was how mad Jack was. And how he stayed out all night." She gulped in a breath. "He got back to the house right before I came to the shop and we didn't speak at all."

"What on earth is all this business about a loan? Y'all aren't hurtin' for money are y'all?"

Dixie looked away from me and said. "I don't want to talk about it right now, Lily Gayle. Not even to you."

Knowing it must be a really big issue if she wouldn't confide in me, I let it go for now. Instead, I hugged her and said into her hair. "Have you seen Jack's boxing gloves today?"

She went stiff in my arms.

"What? His *boxing gloves*? Why?"

"There was a pair of boxing gloves up under the bushes at the crime scene." I told her again, still holding her tight. "I don't want to scare you more. And I truly don't think Jack had anything to do with this. But make sure you find those boxing gloves and put them in a safe place."

Dixie pushed me away and opened the door to go back into the shop.

"Wait a minute, though." I said. "I just had a thought. Those boxing gloves can't be Jack's. He wouldn't have known Tom was up at the Midnight Dragonfly."

"Unless he followed him."

"Wait! What? Followed him?" I hustled in before the door closed and locked me out in the alley. "Why would you *say* that?"

She didn't answer as I skirted around the boxes in her office. Walking so fast I could hardly keep up, Dixie rushed along the short corridor and out into the shop. But her voice was calm when she spoke to the other hairstylist.

"Ashley. I have to run home for a bit. No one's hurt, but I have to do this. Will you please comb out Mildred when her hair gets dry?"

Ashley looked wide eyed at Dixie, then switched her gaze to Mildred. She turned back to Dixie and nodded.

That was all Dixie needed. She headed toward the door at a fast walk. Not even pausing when Mildred stuck her head out from under the dryer and hollered.

I managed to catch up to her outside.

"Hold up. Let's not get crazy here." I panted. "I'm sorry now that I even said anything to you about those gloves. They could be anybody's."

I caught her arm as she started to walk off. "I'm gonna head on over to the the morgue early tomorrow morning. Doc hasn't changed his schedule in years and I know he'll be doing the autopsy then. I'll find out everything I can about the gloves." I promised. "You call me or text when you find them so I know everything's okay with you."

Dixie, mouth in a grim line, nodded as she pulled her car keys from her purse. I knew she'd tear the house apart looking for those gloves. And probably call Jack at work to check if he had them in his car.

I said a little silent prayer as she backed out of the parking space down the street and headed home at a speed above the posted limit.

CHAPTER FIVE

I still hadn't heard back from Dixie the next morning when I made my way to the hospital to visit the morgue in the basement to wheedle any and all information I could from Ben and Doc Johnson.

Jimmy John, aka JJ, my long-time nemesis and the guardian of all who got to go to the autopsy suite at the hospital, stood up from his desk as I entered the building, blocking my way into the autopsy area.

"Now JJ. You know the Doc and Ben will want me in there with them. Why make a big deal out of letting me go on in?" I reasoned.

JJ glared. "I haven't gotten any word from Doc about you being here. And the sheriff isn't here yet. So you best sit yourself down over there in one of those chairs and wait."

I didn't even glance at the two uncomfortable molded plastic chairs that sat across from JJ's desk. No way would I sit down. It annoyed me to no end that JJ was enjoying his little display of authority.

I should've just waited outside till Ben got here and avoided this whole silly scene, but I've never been one to make things easy for myself.

As we stood facing each other like enemies at high noon in a bad western, Ben strode through the doors. He squinted like he didn't recognize me. But I knew him better than that. Sure as God made little green apples he was deciding which argument to use on me to keep me out. And I wasn't having that. Not with JJ as a witness.

As luck would have it, Doc Johnson hustled out of his office midway down the hall and hollered, "Howdy, Sheriff. Y'all come on back." as he went on to the autopsy room.

Ben and I glared at each other for a quick minute, but as soon a JJ opened his mouth to say something, Ben jerked his head for me to follow him as he strode on down the hallway. Ben might say some harsh things to me about being nosey, but he wouldn't stand for anyone else doing it.

Hard as it was for me, I kept my mouth shut and my eyes on the floor as I followed. No smart remarks. No triumphant smiles. No sense in getting anybody riled at this point in the proceedings.

As soon as we'd cleared the double doors and met up with Doc, Ben started in. "There is *no* reason for Lily Gayle to be here. She's not part of your medical staff and she sure as shootin' isn't part of law enforcement around here. Even though she seems to think she is."

So much for thinking it would be easy thing morning now that I'd got past the front desk on Doc's invitation.

"Come on, Ben." Doc said, looking amused. "You know she's gonna find out any way. And at least if she gets her information here it'll be right. You know how everything gets exaggerated all the time. Like that old game the kids used to play with the tin cans and string."

I almost laughed. Nobody a generation younger than Ben and me would have a clue what the doc was talking about. But, be that as it may, it looked like I'd got my way. I worked real hard at looking demure and grateful.

I'm pretty sure Ben wasn't buying it.

With a deep sigh and a put upon look, he moved to the table where poor old Tom Hammond was laid out. Doc had a sheet pulled up to Tom's chin giving him what little dignity could be had at this point in the proceedings.

Pulling a pair of cheaters from the breast pocket of his lab coat, Doc perched them on the end of his nose and read from a manila folder in his hand.

"The victim arrived at the Mercy Hospital emergency room with a very low pulse and faint heartbeat. His fingertips were blue and his pupils were pinpoints. We considered having him air lifted to the trauma center in Memphis, but felt that he would not make it that far and attempted to save him here on site. The tox screen indicated a high level of alcohol and a hypnotic sedative that we've since identified as Ambien."

Doc shuffled the page aside and read some more as Ben and I stood silent. No doubt Ben was mentally processing the information just like I was. I mean I'm no medical expert, but it sure sounded like ol' Tom has partied pretty hard at the Christmas party earlier that night.

It kinda surprised me, truth to tell. I never would have pegged Tom as indulging in excess. He was wound so tight all the time I ever saw him and he kept a tight rein on Patsy, too. Why he never let her go anywhere without him in the last several years.

That would never fly for me, but Patsy'd always been a little different. Even when she was a little girl.

And what about the Ambien? Who takes a sleep aid before heading out to a Christmas party? Or had he taken it later that night trying to get to sleep up at the Midnight Dragonfly? Didn't make sense to me at all.

Ben shifted beside me making his leather gun belt creak in the quiet room and pulled me out of my thoughts.

Doc's eyes scanned some pages in his folder then he said, "There were several needle marks found on the victim's inner arm. Ben, do you know if he'd been admitted to the sleep study earlier that night?"

Ben scratched his head. "As a matter of fact he had been checked in just before midnight. Then Vlad found him out on the porch unconscious the next morning and called 911. No idea how Tom got there or how longed he'd been laying there."

"So. He checked in to the study after the Christmas party?" Doc asked.

"I know." Ben said. "I thought it was pretty odd myself. But Vlad said Tom banged on the door until he answered. Then insisted on being checked into the study right then. Vlad tried to talk him out of it, but couldn't and just gave up and let Tom on in. The study hasn't actually started yet. He put

Tom in one of the rooms for the night and decided they'd figure out the details at a more decent hour. He did go ahead and take some blood samples. He thought he heard something outside later, went downstairs to take a look around and that's when he found Tom on the porch."

Scratching at a small patch of facial hair he'd apparently missed while shaving, he went on. "When I talked to Patsy, she said Tom insisted that he wanted to go ahead and get checked in to the study and she couldn't talk him out of it. So she drove him up there, then went on home. I'm going to be talking to her some more when I leave here. She was in a bad way earlier and I wanted to give her some time to pull herself together. As much as possible under the circumstances, anyway."

With a puzzled look, Doc flutter his fingers through the pages in the folder. "I didn't know they drew blood for a sleep study program."

Ben nodded. "You're right. It's a little unusual. But Vlad's study is one that runs a DNA test for a particular gene that's found in people who have insomnia. At least that's what he told me. I can double check with some other clinics if you think I need to."

Doc leaned against the table holding Tom. "You know. Now that you mention that I believe I read something about it in a journal a few years back." He chuckled. "Mercy seems like an odd place to be conducting high tech studies like that though."

Ben nodded agreement. "Vlad told me he specifically wanted to do the study in a small town because he wants to try to study more than one generation in a family to check for the gene and small towns are more likely to have several generations living in them."

"Well, *that's* for sure." I threw in.

Ben glanced over like he'd forgotten I was there and I regretted the comment. But I'd been here this long. No point in him trying to keep any of it from me now.

"Hm. Interesting angle to study several generations of a family to isolate a particular gene. Smart, too. You could find siblings without it. A parent with it and one without. Fascinating. I'll have to be sure and make friends with Vlad. I'd love to know all the details of the study." He flipped through more pages in the folder, then went on. "There's only a couple more things I wanted to pass along to y'all....I mean *you*, Ben." Doc said as he caught the frown on Ben's face.

"There was a new bruise that had just started forming at the time of death. So I'd say he fell on something or bumped hard into something close to the time he collapsed. His kidney was pretty badly bruised."

Remembering the boxing gloves lying on the ground nearby that night, my interest peaked. "Or maybe someone hit him?"

Doc thought it over for a minute. "Well. It's a pretty large bruise to be made by a fist."

Ben turned his face toward me and mouthed. *Shut up.*

Oops! Guess he didn't want the boxing gloves to become common knowledge. He must be planning on keeping that piece of information secret from the public to help weed out any false information. I couldn't figure out why he wouldn't want *Doc* to know. But, since I didn't want to rile Ben up, I shut up.

Glancing between the two of us, Doc smiled. "If I find out anything else, I'll give you a call, Ben."

"Preciate it, Doc." Motioning me toward the door, he said. "Let's go, Lily Gayle."

As we exited the hospital, Ben stepped over to the side of the building, grabbed my bicycle, pushed the button on his key fob to open the trunk and stored my bicycle there, securing the trunk lid with a bungee cord since it wouldn't close all the way with my bike in there.

He smiled and escorted me to the passenger side of his cruiser, opened the door and motioned me in. Well. This was a nice change. I'd been mentally figuring out my game plan for how to get him to take me to Patsy Hammonds house with him.

When he took a left at the stop sign, I knew what he was up to.

"Now listen here, Ben. I need to go to Patsy's with you."

He pressed harder on the gas pedal. "No. You don't. You've been up in police business enough today already. I'm taking you home."

He pulled into my driveway, cut the engine, got out and retrieved my bike from his trunk. He rolled the bike to the front of my house and leaned it against the porch rail.

I powered the window down, letting in a rush of cold December air. "Hey. Move the bike. You're crushing Mamaw Waddell's rose bush. I reckon it doesn't look like much this time of the year, but she'll come back and haunt you if you kill it."

Looking annoyed, he picked up the bike and took it up on the porch. Where I'd have to carry it back down from when I got ready to ride it again. Payback would be due soon. But not today. He wouldn't trick me out of the car that easily.

Seeing I wasn't getting out, he strode back to the car. Opened the door. Stood looking at me.

I raised one eyebrow.

He motioned me out of the car.

I ignored him.

Through tight lips he said. "Don't make me drag you out of there, Lily Gayle."

I smiled. "You're not scaring me even a little bit with that hollow threat. I know you were raised better than that."

As he leaned toward me, I calmly snapped my seatbelt. Just in case it turned out not to be a hollow threat.

CHAPTER SIX

I tried to keep the satisfied grin off my face as we rode along to Tom and Patsy Hammond's house. I'd won the internal bet I'd made. Ben was too much of a gentleman to manhandle me out of the car.

But, judging by the sour look on his face, he still wasn't happy I'd called his bluff.

I shimmied in the seat trying to get into a comfortable position. The old police cruiser didn't have much plush on the seats. I'm sure Ben thought that was a good thing for a sheriff's car, but it sure made travel hard on the butt.

"Well, this oughtta be pretty interesting." I commented into the silence. Ben didn't so much as turn his head to acknowledge me. "Tom had such a stranglehold on every little thing she did, I don't know how's she's gonna manage by herself."

Still no reaction. "Why I bet she doesn't even know how to pay a bill."

"Why are you being so mean about her?" Ben scolded.

That took me aback. I sighed as I thought it over. "You're right. I have no call to be talking about her like that. She just rubs me the wrong way and I can't even tell you why."

Ben slowed a bit as we went into a turn on a newly graveled road. But the back end fishtailed just a bit anyway. Ben shot me an apologetic look, knowing my issues with car accidents.

"Sorry, Lily Gayle. I didn't mean to do that."

I loosened my death grip on the oh-shit handle above the door. "No harm." I said. But I wiped sweaty palms on my pant legs to get rid of the moisture coating them.

Even all these years after my husband had died in a car accident I couldn't quite achieve a state of nonchalance about even the most minor issue in a moving vehicle.

"Were y'all friends in school?" Ben changed the subject. "I don't seem to remember her much."

I looked at him in astonishment. "You seriously don't remember that ridiculous invisible friend she had? The one she swore was her identical twin?"

He guffawed. "Oh, yeah. That was her?"

"You better believe it." I thought it over for a minute. "Maybe me not liking her goes all the way back to elementary school."

We turned in at the Hammond's driveway. At the end sat a neat ranch-style house with a single carport. I would've thought the manager of the local bank would've had a nicer place than this.

Especially since Tom Hammond liked to act like he was better than everyone else in town. I didn't get out this road much and it was the first time I'd seen where the Hammond's lived.

The only car sitting under the carport was the Lexus I'd seen Tom driving around town. At that point it occurred to me to wonder if Patsy had any family or friends to help her out right now. And how awful was that? If it'd been anybody else in town I'd've been over here like a shot with food and a shoulder.

Ben pulled the cruiser to a stop right behind the other car and turned to me. "We need to get her to give up the punch bowl and glasses so I can get them to the lab for testing and fingerprinting." He pushed a hand through his hair. "I should have got over here already to do that. I just hope she hasn't already washed them yet."

I shot Ben an incredulous look. "Are you serious? *That's* why were over here?" I laughed. "You do know we're talking about Patsy Hammond, right? The woman who is always perfectly dressed and has her perfectly decorated home perfectly clean at all times."

Ben glanced over at me, amused. "Do I detect a note of sarcasm there?"

"Of course not." I answered. "*Everyone* thinks Patsy is over the top with all her neat freak doings." And there went the guilty feelings I'd had just a minute ago.

"I thought y'all aren't friends."

I gave him a look that said *And you're point would be?*

He went on. "If y'all aren't friends, how do you know her house is perfect?" Ben widened his eyes. " Are you telling me that you're relying on rumor and conjecture?"

I gave him a dirty look as I released my seatbelt and opened my door "Come on. I feel sure they've been washed, polished and put away, but it's worth a try. And, it's a good thing I came with you. I doubt she'd let you have the punch bowl and cups if I wasn't here."

Ben got out and met me at the front of the car. "Why not?"

"Well. We aren't friends or anything but everyone in town knows that set belonged to her grandmother and she's real particular about it."

As we went up the brick walk to the front door, Ben replied. "If it's that special to her, why does she loan it out for the Christmas party? I'd be scared to death someone would drop one of the cups or something. And, even more of a mystery, why will she let me have it just because you're with me? Y'all aren't even friends according to you."

As he knocked on the door, I told him. "Two things. It's a woman trust thing and she's an odd duck. That'll have to cover it."

Hearing footsteps approaching on the other side of the door I added. "And I believe you're here to ask questions about why Tom insisted on signing in to the sleep study so late at night. You're just using the punch bowl set as a cover excuse."

I turned as the door opened and couldn't have been more shocked if someone had punched me. The Patsy who answered the door bore not the slightest resemblance to the put together woman I always saw at church and at the grocery store with Tom.

This Patsy's hair straggled in a mess around her face. A face blotched with mascara stains and smeared makeup. And what the heck did she have on? It looked like a quilted robe with strings dangling all over it. It should've been thrown in the trash heap a long, long time ago in my opinion. Ben's eyes, when he turned them to me, echoed my thoughts. This was a woman that needed some assistance. And needed it now. All my guilty feelings rushed right back in."

"Patsy. You poor thing!" I put my arm around her and turned us back into the house. I headed toward the living room with her, but she dug her feet in and turned us toward the kitchen. I got her in a chair at the table and pulled up the one next to her.

"I am so sorry I haven't been by before now, hon."

Patsy looked at me out of suspicious eyes. As well she might. She knew I didn't like her. But, gosh darn it, she was a mess.

"Have you had anything to eat?" I asked. When she shook her head I jumped up and went to the refrigerator. I might not be a gourmet cook, but I can scramble eggs with the best of them. And you could always count on people having eggs on hand.

"Don't!" Patsy said in a harsh voice. I nearly dropped the eggs right on the floor I was so startled.

"You need to get some food in you, hon."

"I don't want any food. I couldn't eat a thing." Patsy traced her fingers over an embroidered placement on the table. I wondered if she'd been the one to do the embroidery.

After putting the eggs back in the refrigerator, I sat at the table. Ben shuffled over and sat across from us. Silence dragged on for a minute, then Patsy said.

"Y'all are here about Tom. Aren't you?"

Ben cleared his throat. "Yes, Patsy. We are." He shifted in his chair, rubbed his hand across his head. "I know I already talked to you about Tom being at the sleep study. But some evidence has come to light and I was wondering if you could let me take your punchbowl and cups into the office."

Patsy stared at Ben from distant eyes. "My granny's punch bowl set?" She frowned. "Why would you need that?"

"I need to test it for residue."

Patsy's fingers traced the pattern on the place mat faster and faster, almost as though she were reading braille, as she kept her eyes on Ben. "Residue? You think there was something in the punch?"

Ben held up a hand. "Now, Patsy. Don't be getting upset. It's part of the investigation is all."

Emotion flared in Patsy's eyes. "If you think there was something in the punch I have a right to know." Her fingers moved to pulling strings on her robe. "My husband is dead. And somebody murdered him. I have a right to know everything you know."

I reached over, rubbing Patsy's back, trying to soothe her. She shook my hand off. "You stop it, Lily Gayle Lambert. I know you're not my friend so quit pretending."

She turned her eyes back to Ben. "And *you*. You better be finding who killed by husband. And be right quick about it, too. I saw Miss Edna give Tom a glass of punch at the Christmas party. Are you questioning *her*?" Patsy leaned forward. "You'd best be questioning Jack Newsom, too. I saw him out driving the roads by himself after I dropped Tom off up at the sleep study. He looked mad as a hornet." She paused, then went on. "And I know Tom turned him down for a loan a few days ago. Tom said Jack was pretty upset about gettin' turned down. Felt like he was being treated wrong."

I bristled. Who did she think she was trying to put blame on Jack? Ben caught my eye and gave me a warning look. I clamped my mouth tight shut, but my thoughts stayed dark.

"And what about that sleep study?" Patsy ranted on. "That's the strangest thing I ever heard of. And that doctor. Tom said he used to live here when he was a kid. And that he lived at Mitchell Manor with his parents. Knowing what we do now about the Mitchells, that guy could be as crazy as they were. Why, he could've killed Tom after I left."

Ben made calming motions with his hands. Guess he was scared to touch Patsy after she'd jumped all over me about it.

"Now, Patsy. If you were concerned about the sleep study, why did you take Tom up there and drop him off?"

Patsy sniffled. The woman could run a range of emotions faster than anyone I ever met.

"Tom is so hard headed." She paused with more tears gathering in her eyes. "I mean *was* so hard headed. You couldn't tell him anything. He had it in mind to participate in that study and there wasn't anything I could do to talk him out of it. So I drove him up there."

"Did y'all have words between you before you took him up there, Patsy?" Ben asked in a calm voice. "Doctor Templeton said he felt like the two of you weren't happy with each other when he saw y'all."

"Well, I *never*!" Patsy snapped. "Are you taking the word of some *stranger* over mine, Sheriff?"

"Of course not. I'm sorry as I can be, Patsy." Ben commiserated. "I'll find the killer as fast as I can. You have my word."

Patsy nodded, pulled a crumpled tissue from a pocket somewhere in that tattered robe and dabbed her eyes.

"I'm sorry I got so riled up, Ben. I know you'll do everything you can."

Ben shifted in his chair. He'd never been good a taking a compliment of any kind. And I knew he didn't have a clue about what to do for Patsy right now. Time for me to intervene.

"Patsy." I said in a quiet voice. "Did you wash up the punch bowl and glasses after the party?"

Startled, she turned her gaze to me. "Normally, I would have washed them up right away."

I nodded agreement and encouragement. Hope blossomed.

"But, with what happened to Tom, I just put them in the pantry all dirty. I couldn't face cleaning them up. My granny would be so put out with me. I was raised better."

"That's okay, Patsy." I risked putting my hand over hers and didn't get it bit off. "As a matter of fact it's the best thing you could have done. Right, Ben?"

Ben smiled. "Why, Patsy, that's great news. I'll be able to take them in and run some tests that might help us find out who killed Tom."

Patsy smiled. "Well. Okay then. I reckon I can let you take them." She stood and moved to a door set in the kitchen wall. Inside was a stack of dirty crystal cups next to a matching punch bowl.

In no time Ben had loaded the delicate set into a box I found in the closet and we were on our way back to town.

"So much for your sisterhood of women being the reason she'd let me have the evidence."

I grimaced. "Well. I *did* tell you Patsy Hammond is a strange duck didn't I? Did you notice that range of emotions going on in there?"

"Her husband got murdered. Do you think you'd be any better under the circumstances?"

CHAPTER SEVEN

As soon as Ben and I got back to town, I called Dixie and set up for us to go out to Patsy's after the shop closed. We'd take food for Patsy so she wouldn't have to be cooking for herself.

I may not like her much, but I couldn't stand to think of her out there by herself with nothing to eat. Dixie said she'd call Miss Edna to get the food donations started and we'd go around picking up the various offerings and take them with us.

By six in evening we were in Dixie's car with a back seat full of casseroles heading to Patsy's house. At this time of year darkness had descended so we drove carefully on the country roads.

"I feel just awful that I've been so caught up in my own worries that I didn't think to go out here already." Dixie lamented as she slowed for the curve where Ben'd fishtailed earlier today. Darn gravel roads. When new gravel sets put down it takes a few days for it to settle and makes it a whole lot easier to slide into the ditches on each side.

"I know. I thought I'd cry myself when she opened the door to Ben and me."

Dixie glanced at me doubtfully.

"I know I've never had much use for her" I admitted. "But to see her in that condition when she's always prided herself on looking perfect really struck home with me."

At Dixie's continued doubtful look, I crossed my arms and sat back. "Where is the Sam hill is Tom's sister, I want to know? Why isn't she here already?"

Dixie drove on, her face ghostly in the lights from the dash. After a minute she said. "You know. I can't remember seeing her in years. She left town after high school, but it seems like she used to come back every now and then."

I stared into the dark countryside sliding past the car windows and thought back myself. Tom's sister, Lisa, had graduated from high school two years before Dixie and me. She'd left town on a basketball scholarship to one of the Kentucky colleges.

It seemed like she'd come home for Tom and Patsy's wedding. I squinted trying to concentrate. And – maybe – when Tom'd been promoted to manage the local bank branch. But, try as I might, I couldn't conjure up any other memories of her.

"Lisa may be on her way. We can ask Patsy just to be sure she won't be out here alone trying to plan the funeral. And if she needs help, I know you'll bend over backwards to make sure she gets it." Realizing that'd come out a bit snarky, I added. "Because you're so good at taking care of people. Unlike me."

She laughed. "You're not so bad at it. You made calls today as soon as you realized Patsy needed help."

We rode in companionable silence for a mile or so, gravel popping under the tires. Soft oldies rock playing on the radio filling the car with memories.

"So, want to tell me about this bank loan business?" I asked softly, thinking, in the cover of darkness, and in our current mood, she might be a little more open to telling me what was going on.

She stayed quiet for another minute, then sighed deep. "Josh lost his scholarship at Ole Miss and we don't have the money to pay his tuition. We don't want him to drop out 'cause we're scared he won't ever go back."

Shocked, I asked. "What happened?"

Dixie's grip tightened on the steering wheel as her lips went thin. "He got over there to Oxford and got so busy having a good time he quit going to classes. Now he's flunking out and his scholarship has been withdrawn. When he comes home next week for Christmas break that's it unless we can come up with the money for next semester."

Cacophonous just about covered the sound of Dixie's dreams crashing to the ground. Josh was the apple of his mama and daddy's eyes. The miracle baby they thought they'd never have. Dixie'd come up pregnant at thirty-two after she'd been told all her life she'd never have children.

As a result, they'd given him everything. But he'd always been a great kid in spite of all that. He'd won a full academic scholarship to Ole Miss, my alma mater, and had gone off determined to do his parents proud as the first in his family to attend college. I knew it meant everything to Dixie and Jack.

"Oh, Dixie." I whispered. "I'm *so* sorry."

"So's Josh." Dixie answered in a bleak tone. "But that don't change anything. It looks like this could be the end of the line for our dreams for him." She gave a laugh with a hysterical edge to it. "Now you understand why I'm worried sick about Jack going missing all night the same night Tom Hammond got murdered." She turned a pale face to me. "And Jack's boxing gloves are missing."

I gulped, overcome by a total loss of words.

At that moment, the car headlights lit up the Hammond house with only one small light shining in a front window. The porch and carport in shadows. If I didn't know better I'd think no one was at home.

"Come on." Dixie gave me a trembly smile. "Let's go take care of Patsy. She's in worse shape than I am. And it'll give me something else to focus on for a bit."

I expected the porch light to click on after we pulled armfuls of casseroles packed into carriers out of the car and slammed the car doors. But not a sound came and not a light flashed on.

We picked our carefully way across the yard, trying not to trip over shadows in the dark and eased up to the front door. Juggling my casseroles around enough to free one hand, I knocked hard. Maybe Patsy'd laid down and gone to sleep or something.

Still no sounds of movement or lights coming on. Dixie frowned. I leaned on the doorbell and stayed there listening to it jangle through the house for a full five minutes before the front door finally sucked open and Patsy glared out at us. The porch light flicked on showing Patsy in the same disheveled state she'd been in earlier today. The minute she realized Dixie was standing there, her expression changed.

Pushing open the security door, she exclaimed. "Why Dixie Newsom! What brings you out here this evening?"

The fakeness just about killed me. After she'd all but accused Jack of killing her husband, here she was falling all over herself to welcome Dixie.

Dixie bustled on into the house, but I gave Patsy a close once over as I passed her on my way in.

"Lily Gayle." She said in a flat voice. "How nice of you to come all the way back out here." She glanced around outside like she was checking to see if anybody else was out there, then shut and dead bolted the front door.

I followed Dixie out to the kitchen where she was busy loading casseroles into the refrigerator. Hefting my load of casseroles onto the kitchen table

I flexed my arm and hand where they'd gone a bit numb from carrying so much weight at one time.

What in the world could be in those carriers that weighed so much? Probably the dishes themselves. Folks around here tended to use glass instead of plastic or aluminum casserole pans these days.

Patsy came in and sat at the table, hands in her lap, head bowed. She looked like a lost child sitting there like that. "I appreciate all the food." She said into her lap. "Y'all didn't need to bring it out here tonight, though. I'm fine right now."

Dixie turned from her task and gave Patsy a long look. "Well, hon. That's how we do things around here. We take care of each other." Touching Patsy on the shoulder, she added. "You know that."

Right then Patsy busted into tears, scaring me half to death. Unfazed, Dixie pulled a chair over to sit next to the crying woman and hugged her close. Patsy put her head on Dixie's shoulder and bawled like a calf lost from its mama.

"What am I gonna *do*?" she wailed. "Tom took care of everything and I'm so lost."

I sat down on the other side of her and took her hand in mine. "You'll do what you have to. And we're here to help you till you can get it all straightened out."

"Thank you, Lily Gayle." She sat up and sniffled. "I'm sorry I was a bit rude to you earlier."

"That's okay, Patsy. You've got a lot on your mind right now. No need for apologies."

Dixie stood up to put the rest of the casseroles into the refrigerator. "There's sure a lot of food here, Patsy. You'll have your choice of a lot of different things to eat."

Patsy blotted more tears from her face with a soggy tissue. "Tom's sister is coming in from Louisville this evening. She couldn't get away before now. We'll be planning the funeral together."

At that moment we all heard the sound of gravel popping. Dixie glanced out the window over the sink. "It's a white SUV."

"That'll be Lisa." Patsy said, standing and scrubbing at her eyes.

Once Lisa'd gotten settled in with Patsy, Dixie and I headed on back to town.

"Poor Patsy." Dixie sympathized as we drove away. "I'd be the same kind of mess if something happened to Jack."

This wasn't a path I wanted to walk down just now. My own husband had died in a car accident ten years ago. I still don't drive. Even though Ben and Dixie had been at me to take it up again. Pointing out that I could get run over riding my bicycle and hurt more than likely hurt worse than if I was in a car.

Thinking about the past brought me back around to Vlad. I hadn't gotten to talk to him just yet since there'd been a dead body on his front porch when I went up to see him. But it was definitely the Vlad from my childhood.

"The other day when I went up to the Midnight Dragonfly to meet Vlad and see if it was our Vlad I didn't get a chance to talk to him much."

Dixie smiled into the dashboard lights. "So it's our Vlad?"

"Yep. All grown up. And a doctor to boot."

She laughed. "That doesn't surprise me. He always hated being sick and not being able to go to school with all the other kids."

I remembered that pale little boy with the big dark eyes. So earnest in his desire to be just like the other kids. He'd snuck out of Mitchell Manor, the former name of the Midnight Dragonfly, and found Dixie, Ben and me playing in the woods.

After that, we'd met often to play. But always in those woods. Vlad was scared to death to be out in the open. I guess he was scared someone would see him acting like a normal kid.

"Remember those sugar cubes he always had in his pockets?" Dixie asked.

I laughed. "I remember I thought he had a pony hidden somewhere on the Mitchell land and the sugar cubes were for the pony."

Dixie laughed, too. "You were crazy to have a pony back then."

"I sure was. But I never could talk Mama and Daddy into getting me one."

"Well where were you going to keep it?" Dixie asked in a practical voice.

"There are two acres of land with the house you know." I reminded her.

"Yes. But no barn, no hay, no all the stuff that goes along with taking care of a pony."

"You sound just like them." I grumbled. "Do you think he's diabetic?"

"Who?"

I frowned at her. "*Vlad*."

"Oh." She drummed her fingers on the steering wheel. "I can't think of any other reason for the sugar cubes. And it seems like he got shots kind of regular, too, back then." As we pulled into my driveway, she said. "Tomorrow night's your family dinner with Ben isn't it."

"Yes. It ought to be interesting. Me trying to drag details of the murder out of him and him trying to make sure I don't find out one little thing more than I already know."

I headed up the steps to meet a disgruntled Elliot meowing loudly on the porch, and heard Dixie's laughter spilling from the car as she pulled out of my driveway.

I picked Elliott up, scratching him under his furry chin as I pressed the code into the modern deadbolt I'd installed on the front door. Yes. Tomorrow night should be interesting.

CHAPTER EIGHT

No matter how much arguing and fussing Ben and I might have going on at any given time, we still have our weekly family dinner together. We're the last of those who'd started the tradition long before we were even born.

I suppose it's just so ingrained that it never occurred to either of us to call a halt to it now that it's only the two of us left.

This week Ben had offered to drive us down to Como, Mississippi to the Como Steakhouse. The best darn steak anywhere in a hundred miles in a lot of people's opinions. Including mine. And a fairly long haul from Mercy down Interstate 55. But I love that place, so the ride's worth it.

On the drive down, Ben dropped a verbal bomb in my lap. Right out of the blue he said, "I want you to know I'm going to arrest Miss Edna for suspicion of murder."

So much for my prediction to Dixie that's it'd be like pulling rusty nails to get any information out of him about the murder. And a good thing I wasn't the one driving 'cause I would sure have driven right off the interstate and into a ditch in someone's pasture land. "What the *hell*?"

Ben calmly clicked the cruise control on the truck and went on. "Now don't get your panties in a twist –"

"You've got a hell of a nerve, Benjie Carter. Telling me you're going to arrest Miss Edna and then telling me not to get my panties in a twist." I swung open handed across the space between us and backhanded him in the chest with my left hand. "Turn this car around and take me home right now."

He ignored my smack. And my order to turn the truck around. As we passed two exits that would have let him take me back home he didn't say a word. Waiting for my curiosity to get the better of me. Darn him. He knew me way too well.

"Fine." I said. "Tell me why you're going to arrest Miss Edna. What evidence do you have?"

I had to give him credit for not having the slightest look of triumph on his face. "I used some county funds to have surveillance cameras installed inside and outside of the depot."

"*What!?*"I gasped, thinking about poor Dixie. Her argument with Jack must have been recorded completely since it happened right outside the depot. "How could you do that and not tell anybody?"

Ben glanced over. "Because the whole point of having them is to catch criminals."

"What criminals? We live in Mercy, Mississippi for God's sake."

Ben sighed. "We've had some problems lately with break-ins at the depot. Nothing destroyed, but someone, probably kids, have broken in and left a lot of trash and such." He gripped the steering wheel tight in both hands. "I want to make sure nothing more serious happens. Nip it in the bud so to speak."

Well. That was a surprise. I had no idea any break-ins had happened. "You could have told *me* about the cameras at least."

Ben grimaced. "And you would have told Dixie. And maybe Miss Edna. And who knows who *they* would have told."

I turned my head, watching the flat pastures and occasional clump of trees stream by outside the car. I wanted to deny that I would have told anyone about the cameras. But, I would have told Dixie. Ben had a point there. But *not* Miss Edna. Well.....probably not Miss Edna. Sometimes I love her to death. But lately I'd been avoiding her except for the weekly breakfast with the girls.

I circled back around to the topic I'd started with. "So, you saw Miss Edna doing something to Tom Hammond at the Christmas party?"

The sign for the Como exit came up and Ben signaled the turn before he answered. "You cannot tell this to *anyone*." He glance over at me as we stopped at the bottom of the exit ramp. "Give me your word."

"Oh for Heaven's sake, Ben."

He stayed quiet.

"Okay. You have my word."

"Swear it."

Annoyed that he'd take it this far, I answered. "I swear on my life that I will not tell anyone anything you tell me about Miss Edna and the cameras."

He raised his eyebrows.

"Really? That's not enough?" I glanced around the interior of his Chevy Avalanche. Popped open the glove box and riffled through the contents. "Do you have a Bible in here somewhere you want me to put my hand on while I swear?"

He ran his hand through his short hair. "I wish I did. I'd sure make you swear on it."

"That's blasphemous." I said indignantly.

"It's done in a courtroom all the time."

"Well." I waved my hands around, narrowly missing his face in my agitation. "This is not a courtroom."

A car came down the exit ramp behind us and Ben took a right turn onto the road that would take us over to the the steakhouse. "You're right." He admitted with a sheepish look. "But I'm dead serious about you keeping this information to yourself."

"I gave you my solemn word." I reminded him.

"When I was looking into Tom's activities prior to finding him there on the porch at the Midnight Dragonfly, I reviewed the cameras from the depot during the Christmas party to see if anything odd turned up on them. And it did."

I snorted, but didn't interrupt.

"I saw Miss Edna talking to Tom Hammond, then take his punch glass, go over to the punch bowl, refill it and add something to it."

"And no one else saw this happen?" I asked sarcastically. "The place was full from what I could see."

He gave me a hard look. "Yes. I saw you on the outside cameras. But, strangely, never on the inside ones."

I winced. "You got me. I went there with every intention of going in. But, then I saw Dixie and Jack arguing and....well....I just decided to go on home instead of going in."

Ben drove around the town square looking for a parking place. There wasn't much in Como so parking was pretty limited. As we circled the block again, Ben went on.

"I went back to Doc Johnson after I watched the video. In a chain reaction event, Marlene bumped into Tom right after Miss Edna brought his refill of punch and some of it splashed on his shirt. I asked Doc to see if there was any way he could test that spot and tell me what it was."

I scanned the town square trying to spot a parking space as Ben slowed to a crawl for a spot that turned out to have a motorcycle in it.

"Doc took a close look at the stain under a microscope and thought it looked oily. Since Miss Edna is from a generation that used castor oil to treat a bunch of stuff, he took a chance that it might be that and tested for it. The test came back positive."

"Look. Someone's backing out up there. Let's get that spot."

Ben pulled the truck up close to the car backing out. Once it cleared the space, I saw another car coming in from the opposite direction with the obvious intention of grabbing the spot before we did. But they didn't know Ben. He was a master of maneuvering his truck and squeezed past the car that was leaving with only a hair between the two vehicles. The other driver had the audacity to honk at Ben.

Ben whipped out the bubble light he kept in the truck in case an emergency came up when he wasn't in his cruiser, placed it on the dash and turned it on. Blue light flashed out into the square, but no sirens.

The other car moved on. A bit faster than strictly was wise, but Ben wasn't going to write the guy a ticket. We were out of Barkley County and Ben didn't have jurisdiction here.

"That was mean." I said around my laughter at the look on the other driver's face as he sped away.

Ben laughed, too. Looking more like the carefree cousin I'd grown up with than he had in a while.

"Come on" He said. "Let's go put our name on the list. Looks like we might have a wait ahead of us."

As we walked toward the steakhouse amidst a slew of Christmas decorations festooning the restaurants and the square itself, I saw clumps of people standing around on the sidewalk chatting and a glance through the windows framed with twinkling Christmas lights revealed the inside seating to wait for a table filled shoulder to shoulder.

"After we give our names to the hostess, let's go upstairs to the bar and have a drink while we're waiting." I said.

"Sure. If we can get a seat up there." He pointed toward the second story patio. "Looks like there's a passel of folks already up there. It's pretty chilly to be sitting outside, so the tables inside must be full up."

I shrugged. Maybe we'd luck out and get the table, or at least the chairs, of someone being called downstairs to dinner.

The hostess told us we'd have a thirty to forty-five minute wait. Pretty standard for a weekend night at the Como Steakhouse. Ben told her we'd be waiting up in the bar and she wished us luck with finding a table.

Once we got upstairs, the inside of the bar was even more crowded than the outside patio. But we managed to snag a table the size of a dinner plate with two wonky chairs tucked into a corner.

Pulling my feet as close to the chair as possible to avoid tripping anyone, I said to Ben.

"Getting back to Miss Edna and the castor oil. Does Doc Johnson think it contributed to Tom dying?"

Ben cleared his throat, looking pointedly around the room full of people.

"Seriously?" I said. "You think anyone else can hear what we're saying in all this racket?" I held my hand up to cup my ear. "I can hardly hear you and I'm sitting a foot away."

"Doc said he thinks the cause of death is the Ambien – combined with the alcohol in the punch. We're still waiting on some results to come back on some more extensive testing than what was done in the Mercy ER."

Just then I faintly heard Ben's name being called and looked up. The hostess from the restaurant was at the door waving to get our attention. We followed her downstairs to our table and placed our orders with the waitress.

Once she left, I turned the topic of conversation back to the murder.

"If Doc doesn't think the castor oil contributed to Tom's death, why are you hell bent on arresting poor Miss Edna?"

Ben said. "Even though he doesn't think Tom died because Miss Edna put all that castor oil in his punch, it *might* have contributed to it...according to Doc." He took a sip of his wine. "I told you we're still waiting on some more test results."

I felt pretty sure Ben was exaggerating what Doc had said about the castor oil. Fuming, I waited quiet as a mouse as our waitress put our steaks to the table. Shook my head about needing anything else. I didn't trust myself to speak with a civil tongue right now.

Once she was gone, I took out some of my frustration on my steak. Cutting it quickly with the sharp knife. But I couldn't keep quiet for long. It's just in my nature.

"Land sakes, Ben. You know as well as I do that the castor oil is not important to this case." I stabbed a piece of my filet and ate it. Chewing in frustration. But the taste of it calmed me down. It was superb. Almost melting in my mouth.

Ben pushed his plate to the side and leaned on the table. "Miss Edna tried to poison a citizen in my town. And she needs to understand the consequences."

"Oh stop it. That's ridiculous. She wouldn't try to *poison* anybody."

"Have you heard of ricin?" Ben interrupted.

I stopped, startled by the unrelated question and tried to figure out why he was asking it.

Ben went on. "Well. Speechless for once."

I opened my mouth to give him a piece of my mind when he waved his hand around.

"Don't get in a tizzy. I'm going to tell you why I asked about ricin. It's made from castor beans."

I thought I might come over in a faint right there at the table as the blood drained from my head at what he implied. And he took advantage of my continued silence.

"I grant you, that ricin is not in castor oil. It's a byproduct of processing the beans into the oil."

I glared at him for getting me so upset.

"But the fact of the matter is that I don't want anyone in my town playing around doing what Miss Edna pulled. If I don't make an example of her and it gets out that she dosed Tom with castor oil to give him a case of the shits – and I'm assuming *that* was her intention -- kids may decide that it's fun to do stuff like that and the next thing you know there's a stream of people in the emergency room." He downed the rest of the wine in his glass and thumped it on the table. "I won't stand for it in my town."

I sat silent for a minute. Willing myself not to say it. Biting my cheeks. Pinching my thigh under the table. But I couldn't resist.

"You mean a shit storm?"

Ben blew out a puff of air. "Will you be serious for one minute?"

But I could see him struggling not to laugh. I waited. And got my reward. He burst out laughing loud enough to draw the attention of everyone in the restaurant.

CHAPTER NINE

After my dinner with Ben the night before I wasn't as surprised as I might have been when Glen Miller started playing on my phone mid-morning. Miss Edna's ringtone. Ben must have gone through with arresting her.

I was pure-D mad about it. He knew as well as I did that Miss Edna putting some castor oil in his punch didn't kill Tom Hammond. I mentally called Ben every name in the book as I reached for my phone.

"Hey, Miss Edna."

"Lily Gayle. I need you to come on over here to the jail and bail me out."

Bail her out?

Ben had really gone whole hog on this. I couldn't figure out what grounds he was using to make her have to post bail. There was no way an eighty-year-old woman would be going on the lam. Why hadn't he just released her on her own recognizance?

"Lily Gayle!" Miss Edna interrupted my internal pondering.

"Oh. Yes, ma'am. I'll be right over."

No matter that I'd been avoiding her lately. I wouldn't leave her at the jail for anything. Clicking off my phone, I stuck it in my back pocket, locked the door behind me and hopped on my bike. With the cold December wind chapping my face, I tucked my chin into my scarf and thought about trying to drive again.

Half an hour later, as I walked Miss Edna home in the cold air pushing my bike, she complained bitterly. "I cannot *believe* I had to ask you to post bail to get me out of jail. I've known Ben Carter since he was in diapers. He has some nerve arresting me on murder charges!"

Matching my steps to her short ones with her walker I answered. "Ben said you went in there and confessed." Before Miss Edna had gotten released from the jail cell I'd had some sharp words with Ben about him making her post bail and he'd said Miss Edna had to learn a lesson about having respect for other people.

I snorted at that thought and told Ben he was taking his authority over the limit by his actions in this.

The old woman grunted. "I did no such thing. I thought I being asked to come in to give evidence as a witness at the party that night. So, I went in there and gave Ben information about the deceased that I thought he could use to solve the crime. Not to arrest *me*."

She stopped and turned to face me. "Why the sheriff had a notion he was gonna put one of those ankle bracelets on me that would let him know if I left my house." She pounded a fist on her walker. "I let him know right quick that no such thing was gonna happen. Why, my word has been good enough for everyone in this town my whole life! It ridiculous I have to be under house arrest anyway.

I don't aim to do anything to anybody else. I got my revenge and I'm done."

"So it really was castor oil and you put it in Tom's drink on purpose? Why?"

Miss Edna grinned a grin that would have made the Grinch proud. "As soon as I saw him doing the butt clinch walk in the direction of the men's room I knew my job was done. So I headed on home."

With a frown she continued. "After Tom Hammond talked about Harley Ann being a murderer and in prison for it so there was no way a reputable bank like his would loan her any money I saw red for a week. I tried explaining to him that she was duped by a bad man, had served her time and shouldn't be penalized forever for it, but Tom wouldn't have any of it. I was mad as a wet hen. But I didn't kill him."

"*You* asked Tom Hammond for a loan?" I said in disbelief.

"I asked on behalf of Harley Ann. She has an idea for a business. A good idea. But Tom Hammond got nasty with me about a loan for her."

"It's Ben's *job* to find out who killed Tom." I thought over what Tom had said to Miss Edna as grounds to refuse the loan. I could sympathize with her anger. I didn't even know the girl all that well and I felt furious on her behalf. How was she supposed to get a new start in life?

I decided not to tell Miss Edna what Ben had told me about the concealed cameras that'd been installed in and around the depot. No telling what she'd say about that. She'd be up on her high horse about spying for days if she knew that's how Ben had spotted her putting something in Tom Hammonds punch glass.

Once we got to Miss Edna's house I settled her in her chair in her front room. Harley Ann swept in and hugged her aunt, tucking a blanket around her shoulders and adjusting pillows. I watched, astonished. Miss Edna hated to be treated like an old lady.

"Oh, Aunt Edna! I was so worried." She turned to me. "Thank you, Lily Gayle. I don't know what we would have done without you." The poor girl stood shaking like a leaf. I realized she was probably having flashbacks to her own legal issues and I wanted to beat Ben to a pulp even more for causing this girl more anguish.

"Not to worry, Harley Ann." I smiled as I took a seat myself. "Everything is just fine."

Miss Edna caught the young girls hands in her own. "Now Harley Ann. You sit right down and stop all this fussin'. I'm perfectly fine. It'll take a lot more than Ben Carter to scare me more than a minute."

Harley Ann wrung her hands some more, but did sit down.

"Now, Lily Gayle." Miss Edna said. "Since you're here and not ignoring me right this minute I'm going to put this out there."

I opened my mouth to protest. Then shut it. Not point in arguing a point that we both knew to be true.

Satisfied that I'd held my tongue, Miss Edna went on. "About that business idea for Harley Ann."

Harley Ann immediately jumped from her chair. "Aunt Edna. This isn't the time to be discussing all that. We can do that another time. When you're not upset with other things."

Miss Edna threw off the blanket around her shoulders. "Now you look here, missy. I'm not upset about anything except Ben Carter taking privileges with his authority. And that's nothing to do with you."

I almost laughed to see her spitting fire like this. Such a relief to see her acting normal instead of accepting the old lady treatment from her great-niece.

In a voice that shook, Harley Ann asked. "What did you do that caused the sheriff to call you in like that?"

I expected Miss Edna to explode, but she surprised me by speaking in a kind voice.

"Baby girl. Don't fret yourself. I let my pride and anger get the better of me and did something I shouldn't have." Miss Edna grinned at both of us and in her glee tapped the cane she used inside the house against the hardwood floor. "But even so. Even with Ben Carter arresting me. I'd do it again."

Wide-eyed, Harley Ann leaned forward. Hanging on every word. "What did you do, Aunt Edna?"

Miss Edna cackled. And, since I already knew what she had done, and thought it was kinda funny myself, I had a hard time keeping myself from laughing along with her.

"I put a big dose of castor oil in Tom Hammonds punch at the Christmas party. My mama used to give it to us regular when I was a child. It was a miracle cure for everything."

Both of us laughed hysterically, but Harley Ann sat motionless and silent. With a puzzled look on her young face.

Realizing the problem, Miss Edna explained. "Castor oil used to be the best cure mostly for constipation. It'd give you a big case of diarrhea. That's why I said I knew my work was done when I saw Tom doing the butt clench walk to the men's room. A dose of castor oil never killed anybody, though. Does the sheriff think my mama was trying to kill us children with a big case of the poops?"

"Did you tell all this about the loan, and how Tom acted, to Ben?"

"'Course I did. I must say he wasn't very sympathetic." She darted a glance a the girl sitting next to her. "I couldn't let that man talk about my great niece that way. Why he could destroy her brand new start here with all his meanness. And that's what it was. Pure cussed meanness."

Harley Ann's face turned as red as her hair. "Really, Aunt Edna. I expected things to be hard once everybody knew I'd been in jail. You didn't have to do that." She patted the old woman's hand and smiled. "But I'm sure glad you did."

Miss Edna pushed up from her chair. "Come on in the kitchen, Lily Gayle. I want you to try these recipes using her special jams Harley Ann has fixed up. We could use some advice about her setting up a business to sell this stuff. She's thinking about a food truck." Miss Edna shook her head, "What is that completely inappropriate name you want to call it?"

"Jammin'." Harley Ann answered in a calm voice as the three of use walked to the old fashioned kitchen down the hall. I guess she must know by now that most of Miss Edna's mean remarks were meant to cover a soft heart. "Because I'll be usin' my own jam recipes to flavor most of the foods I'm going to serve."

"Makes absolutely no sense to me, but she seems set on it." Miss Edna complained. "Now, Lily Gayle, you be honest about what you think of the food she's puttin' together. You've got a pretty good head for business and I don't. So I want you to advise the girl."

"Aunt Edna. Please." Harley Ann sputtered. Turning to me she said, "Lily Gayle. I don't want to be taking up your time with my problems."

"Hush, girl. Lily Gayle is a business woman herself. I probably should have talked to her bout your business instead of going to that idiot at the bank. But it was because she's been acting all prickly lately and avoiding me that I just did the wrong thing."

A flash of guilt overcame me. I *had* been avoiding Miss Edna. But her next words took the guilt right off my conscience.

"Getting' a little too big for your britches in my opinion. Thinking you don't need the old woman poking her nose in your business and helping you out."

Harley Ann gasped, then placed her hand over her mouth. I wasn't sure if she was horrified or just trying to suppress a laugh. It the big picture it didn't matter anyway. There was a crumb of truth to the words and I prided myself on being honest. With myself. Not with anyone else who might be pointing out any deficiencies of character to me.

"I know you think I've been sticking my nose into things that aren't any of my business." Miss Edna reiterated. "But I say that's just a case of the pot calling the kettle black."

Harley Ann yanked the fifties style refrigerator open a bit harder than necessary, making the bottled condiments in the door rattle together and breaking the gathering tension in the room.

Miss Edna took her eyes off me and I felt my neck hairs lay on back down. Argument averted. I smiled at Harley Ann who gave me an innocent look as she pulled several sealed containers out of the main part of the refrigerator.

Popping the airtight lids, she set them on the counter in front of me. Meatballs with a glaze of some kind. Bread with a red swirl through it. A sliced muffin with jam oozing out of the center.

Taking a deep breath, Harley Ann explained. "The meatballs are homemade and I have paired them with a peach bourbon jam glaze that I created myself. It's going to be served on potato bread sub roll." She pointed the the bread with the red swirl. "This one is all from scratch too. It's got my homemade strawberry jam swirled through the mix and then baked in." She point to the last item on my plate. "A vegan chocolate muffin with peppermint jam flavored icing. I created the icing recipe myself. And vegan because I believe there's a good market for that."

Every item tasted like a little bit of heaven. The sandwich had just a hint of hotness.

"A teeny bit of jalapeno pepper. To give it a little kick on the tongue." Harley Ann explained when I asked.

I don't know squat about vegan, but I knew that chocolate peppermint muffin would be added to my short list of must haves. And the strawberry swirl bread was marvelous, too.

I explained to Harley Ann about my Etsy store for the period dresses and my genealogy research business. Both of which I did from home.

So I don't have experience with trying to get something started like a food truck business. "I can advise you about business bank accounts and things like that. But I have no idea how to go about setting up a food truck business."

Harley Ann fiddled with the dirty forks on the table. "I'm sure appreciative of everything you can help me with, Lily Gayle. The money part is what scares me most. I can work hard to get word out about the food truck." She grinned. "And I know from you and Aunt Edna that the food I'm creating to sell on it is good. Plus, I'm not scared of hard work."

"Well, that's good." I answered. "Because it'll take a whole bunch of that, and patience, to build up a good business."

Harley Ann nodded.

"Have you been to snoop around on the sleep study and that Vlad person?" asked Miss Edna suddenly. Poking her nose in my business. *Again.*

"I've been trying to get up there for two days. To see my old friend. Not *snoop* into anything." I glared at Miss Edna and ignored Harley Ann's grin she was trying to hide behind her hand.

"I don't know about that." Miss Edna put in. Cementing my desire to get out of here before our newfound truce went to hell in a handbasket.

I drained my glass of tea, set it on the table and stood. "I'm going up there right this minute before something else goes off the rails and needs my attention."

CHAPTER TEN

As I coasted my bicycle into the driveway of the Midnight Dragonfly for the second time this week, I got to thinking more about the bright red '65 Mustang I'd put in storage ten years ago. I paid the manager of the storage unit extra to take it for a drive every couple of weeks to keep the motor in good condition. We'd been friends back at Ole Miss and I trusted him to take care of the car for me.

Maybe it was time to bring it to Mercy. And, maybe, start driving again. At least sometimes. Like winter. But only on clear roads. We rarely get snow, but it's not that unusual to get ice on the roads.

Puffing like a steam engine, my breath clouding the December air, I pushed up the last rise in the driveway and coasted to a halt by the front steps, still thinking about that car. Staggering over to the steps, I plopped down on a middle one in relief.

As I sat there in the weak winter sunlight catching my breath, my heart slowing to normal rhythms, I heard the door behind me open and close. I commanded myself to remain still. To be casual. To let go of the puzzle of why my heart rate accelerated again.

After a moment, feet in well-worn brown loafers appeared on my right and the man wearing them lowered himself onto the step next to me. I looked over into the big brown eyes of Vlad. His smile lit up the morning and I couldn't help but return it.

"Well. Hey there, you." He said, leaning back with his elbows on the step above us.

"Hey." I replied, leaning back next to him.

"I thought I might see you sooner than this. The sheriff seemed to think you were going to come visit right away."

I cringed inside. Leave it to Ben to make a total hash out of something. I swear I think he goes out of his way to create awkward situation for me.

"It's weird to associate the words 'the sheriff' with my old pal Benjie Carter." Vlad went on with a laugh. "I was completely surprised when he was the one to get out of the cruiser the other morning."

He glanced sideways at me. "And I was surprised to see *you* ride up the driveway on a bicycle just like you were still twelve years old."

I felt a blush crawl up my neck and onto my face and counted it a miracle that steam didn't rise off me from all that heat in the cold air. Keeping my voice nonchalant, I answered. "Gotta keep the old girl in shape."

He eyed me up and down and smiled. "Looks like it's working."

My blush flamed hotter. What in the world was wrong with me sitting here acting like a moonstruck teenager? Not my style at all.

I sat up, hugging my knees to my chest. "So. Tell me how you came to be a doctor in charge of sleep study in little ol' Mercy, Mississippi. Last time

I saw you, you were heading off to live with an aunt and uncle you didn't even know you had."

As a shadow passed over his face and he looked away, I felt bad for him. It must've been really hard. After a minute he turned back toward me.

"Yes. Aunt Lucy and Uncle George took good care of me. He smiled. "Even though I was a little shit for a long time."

"You were a little boy!"

He laughed. "Thirteen is *not* a little boy." Shrugging, he added. "But I'm really lucky to have had them. They treated me like their own. Even put me through medical school."

He stood and held out a hand to me. "Come on inside. It's too cold to sit out here on the steps even with the sun shining. This marble is freezing my butt."

I took his hand, letting him pull me to my feet. It did feel a lot cooler now that I wasn't exerting myself. And the marble was definitely butt chilling. We went in the big front door to the wood floored double hallway I hadn't seen since the night of the big grand opening of the Inn.

And, as it turned out, the only night opening of the Inn because Dixie and I solved the case of who'd killed Luxen Natolovich in the kitchen of this house that night. I shivered just a little bit. Not from cold. More the goose-walked-over-my-grave kind of shiver. Vlad noticed and raised an eyebrow.

"Unpleasant memories."

"Really." He led me to the big commercial kitchen and motioned me to a small table next to a window looking out back. "Want to talk about it?"

He fixed us both a mug of coffee using the Keurig on the counter. I felt a bit miffed that he didn't even ask me if I wanted – or like – coffee. But when he placed the big mug on the table in front of me and I inhaled that hazelnut scent, I decided to keep any complaints to myself.

I took a small sip. Eyed him over the rim. "Missy didn't tell you about the history before you bought this place?" I paused, thought, then asked. "*Did* you buy it?"

Rotating his mug on the table, watching the coffee swirl, he answered without looking at me. "I heard there'd been a murder." His eyes roamed the kitchen. "Right here in this room." He raised his eyes to mine. "And that you found the dead guy. Sounds like quite the adventure in snooping."

I gulped too much coffee and sputtered. Vlad jumped up, came around the table and whacked me on the back a few times. I motioned him to sit back down. I was okay, but a bit winded.

"Not snooping." I wheezed. "And not nice of you to say that. You don't know anything about it."

He had the grace to look embarrassed. "You're right. I apologize." He shifted in his chair. "It's so odd to be here again. I keep seeing the past laid over the present." He glanced at me again. "And that little girl who loved Nancy Drew and the Hardy Boys."

Slightly mollified, I eased back in my chair and sipped very carefully at my coffee. "I'm gonna let you slide just his once."

Vlad eased back in his chair, long legs stretched out. "To answer your question. I'm leasing the house for the study."

I watched him, seeing in the handsome man sitting with me the young boy I'd been so fond of. "How did you come to get funding to do a sleep study?"

He grinned. "A lot of smooth talking....and some connections I made in medical school and thru my aunt and uncle. They have connections to movers and shakers in the state who helped get the funding in place."

I chuckled. "I remember you were a pretty smooth talker back in the day. Is that why you're doing the study here? Is this home to you even though you've been gone so long?"

He gave me a sidewise glance. "Something like that." He shifted in his chair. "And I needed a town where multiple generations of the same family live so I can do a generational study of DNA of the people participating in the study to see if any, or all, of them have the gene for insomnia."

"Wow." I said, fully impressed. "That sounds like a ground-breaking study."

He shifted again. *Antsy thing, wasn't he?*

"Well. Not really ground-breaking. There've been some studies already on the gene. I'm just trying to advance it via my generational study."

Well, I'm pretty darn impressed." I stood, taking my mug back to the counter with the Keurig. "I'm helping myself to some more of this high dollar government funded coffee."

His chair scraped across the tile as he pushed back from the table, stood and came to the counter. Placing his mug next to mine, he grinned. "Fill er up, please."

Once we'd settled back at the table with our refills, he asked. "So what're you up to these days?"

I spread my arms wide like a circus showman. "What you see before you is a boss lady."

He chuckled. "Who's boss?"

I lowered my arms, cupping my hands around my coffee mug. "Just me. I have a couple of businesses I run from my house."

"Really! What kind of businesses?"

I shrugged. "Nothing so exciting as a medical study. I have an online store where I sell and take orders for custom historical costumes. My customers are mostly re-enactors." I smiled and added. "And I also do genealogy research."

Vlad whistled. "Smart and talented. What a mix." He gave me a crooked smile. "But you always were smart and talented. I have to say I'm surprised to find you still here in Mercy. Weren't you going to leave this place far behind and see the world?"

I put my hand over my eyes to hide the unexpected tears welling up. Pictures of John and me together, laughing and happy, flashed through my head. Then the accident that took him from me. I felt my other hand taken in a kind grip that almost made me cry more.

Vlad said softly. "Lily Gayle. Forgive me. I've hit on a painful subject without even meaning to."

I shook my head still hiding behind my hand.

Vlad squeezed the hand he still held. "When you're ready, why don't you tell me a little more about the genealogy? How does that work?"

Thankful he'd changed the subject, I managed to push the tears back. I smoothed my hair back off my forehead as I raised the hand covering my eyes. Vlad looked back at me with kind eyes. I looked away to hide my eyes from his gaze because I knew they were bloodshot.

Taking a breath, I told him in a voice that wobbled only a little bit. "It can be pretty interesting. Depending on who I'm researching."

"I bet."

Feeling stronger, I went on. "As a matter of fact. I found some pretty interesting stuff about the Mitchells before all that craziness happened up here. Like, all of them were born at home. Right here in this house. And there was a midwife in every generation. And everyone who ever worked for them came from somewhere else." I paused, considering. "It's unbelievable how many secrets were hiding behind the walls of this house for so long."

He tightened his grip on my hand briefly, then let go and sat back, coffee mug in hand. "I saw some newspaper coverage of all that. Who would ever have dreamed all those dark secrets were being kept up here on this hill."

I pressed my fingertips to my temples. All this emotion about the past was giving me the beginnings of a headache. Especially remembering I'd almost been killed in this house twice. "I know. You couldn't make this stuff up. I don't think I would have put it all together without the necklace LizBeth Mitchell gave me."

I frowned. "It tied the Mitchells to the circus lady and everything evolved from there." I gave him a sharp look. "Did you know anything about all that? Back when you lived here as a kid and your parents worked here?"

He pinched the bridge of his nose. "How would I have known anything about it? I was a kid."

"Yeah. I guess they kept you in the dark, too." I sipped some more coffee, frowning because it'd gotten cold while we chatted. I put the mug back on the table. "Do you still carry sugar cubes in your pocket?"

He looked confused, then brightened. "I'd forgotten all about those sugar cubes. No. I don't carry them anymore."

"So, you've got the diabetes under control by now, I guess. It must've been hard when you were a kid. Not getting to go to school with the rest of us. Being sick like that."

He ran a hand through his hair. "Meeting you and Ben and Dixie was the best thing that ever happened to me. Y'all made my life seem almost normal when we played games together in the woods back then. What happened to Dixie? Is she still living here?"

"Um. Yeah." I struggled to get a grip on my emotions when I felt tears burning unexpectedly at the back of my eyes. What on earth was the matter with me acting like this? I never cry in front of other people. Not even Dixie. And to cry in front of an almost stranger, well that really did take the cake. "Never left Mercy. Married Jack Newsom."

I paused and risked taking a look at Vlad. He gazed calmly back at me. Not like I was a freak or like he might be trying to figure out a way to get a crying woman off his hands. My body relaxed a little bit more.

"She married Jack Newsom. You wouldn't know him, but he's a great guy." I shook my head sadly. "They wanted a passel of kids, but the doctors told Dixie she'd never have any. Then they got the surprise of their lives eighteen years ago and they have a son who's at Ole Miss now."

Remembering what Dixie'd told me about that situation almost made me tear up again. What in tarnation was wrong with me?

I exhaled, pushing the emotions away. "So that's about it. You know all the news about me, Dixie and Ben."

Vlad smiled. "And you know mine."

I smiled back. "Reckon I do."

We sat quietly together for a bit, both of us finishing off the coffee. A beam of late afternoon sunlight angled through the window reminding me it'd be dark soon. This time of year, dark came early. I pushed back from the table and said. "I need to get on home. But it's been great seeing you."

A handshake seemed way too formal for someone who'd been such a close friend once upon a time. But a hug didn't feel quite right either.

Vlad shrugged, pulled me against him for a hug so quick it was over before it started and we grinned like idiots.

"Want to meet in the woods at our old place tomorrow morning?" He asked in a teasing voice.

I smiled, looking out the window toward the woods where we'd played together so many times. Wondering if some remnant of our old tree fort might still be clinging to the trees.

As my eyes swept across the yard, my scan was interrupted by a rusty old truck sitting next to a garden shed out back. I leaned in closer to the window to get a better gander at the old thing in the fading light. Surely not. But...

I turned to Vlad. "Is that old banger out there yours?"

He looked chagrined. "Guilty. I use it to run errands. I bought it when I was doing some work upstairs getting the rooms ready for the study. It worked great for hauling. And I never worried I was damaging it, because it's already banged up."

"I saw it parked in the town square the night of the big Christmas party." I put my hands on my hips, narrowed my eyes. "But nobody saw you at the party."

He tucked his head down. "Guilty. I drove into town to go to the party but chickened out at the last minute."

"You weren't sitting in it. No one was."

He flushed. "I was actually fixing sneak back to it when I saw you standing next to it."

"So you hid rather than meeting me?"

"I didn't want our first meeting after all this time to be in the middle of the town square." He confessed.

Just because I'd felt the same way about meeting him again didn't mean I was letting him off the hook on this.

"I saw some boxing gloves in the truck the night of the party."

He glanced away from me.

"Then I saw some boxing gloves under the bushes out front when they hauled poor Tom Hammond off to the hospital."

He furrowed his brows. "What are you asking me, Lily Gayle?"

I twisted my fingers together, noticing I needed a fresh manicure. "Did you drop your gloves out there by accident or something?"

Frowning, he answered. "No. I don't believe I did. But I will tell you that they've gone missing."

I gulped. Was he trying to tell me he'd done something to Tom Hammond? I realized he and I were the only ones here right now. The sleep study hadn't officially started yet. The thought gave me pause.

"Does Ben know your gloves are missing?" I inquired.

He nodded. "Yes. I told him myself. I saw him get those gloves out from under the bushes after the ambulance left and went to my truck to get mine to show him. I don't for a minute think Ben Carter is some dumb country sheriff so I wanted him to know I have a membership up at the gym in Olive Branch and show him my gloves at the same time." He shrugged. "But when I went to the truck to get them, they were gone."

His eyes clung to mine. I wondered if he was daring me to make assumptions. And I didn't know what to think. I'd been crazy about him a long time ago. That boy had been kind of a hero to me. The man was handsome as the devil but I didn't know him at all. *But you want to* mention a tiny voice in my head. *Oh hush up*, I told it.

"Ben asked my why Tom Hammond was here that time of night. He reckoned it wasn't standard procedure to admit someone the study so late. Never mind that they study hasn't officially started just yet."

"And what did you tell him?"

"I told him that it looked like Tom and his wife'd had some kind of disagreement and Tom was hell bent on getting in here right then." He sighed. "So rather than shut the door in his face, I let him on in and took him up to one of the rooms to spend the night. I was going to work out the details the next morning."

"But the next morning he was dead on your front porch. Or close enough."

"Yes." He drew in a long breath. "I don't know when he went out there or why he was out there. I don't know anything at all, I guess."

I waited. He didn't say anything more. Guess he figured I didn't need the details. Like Tom's blood being drawn before they'd said goodnight. Somehow that bothered me. But likely Vlad thought I didn't need that information.

"Okay. Well. I'm going on home now." Good lord. This was awkward as all get out. How had we gotten from teasing about meeting in the woods like old times to this?

Vlad tilted his head toward the door and I followed in silence. When we reached the front door he opened it and said. "Lily Gayle. I realize a lot has happened. A man is dead. And maybe you're thinking I had a hand in it." He reached toward me, then let his hand fall back to his side. "I'm innocent as the day is long. But I guess you'll have to make your own decision on that."

I walked down the steps to my bicycle, feeling his eyes on me the whole way. It took all of my strong willed resolve not to turn around and look back. As I pedaled on back toward home, I decided I'd get on the internet and see what I could find out about Vlad Templeton, the doctor ....and maybe what'd led him to come back to Mercy for his sleep study.

I'd also check my genealogy sites to see what I could come up with on his family.

Not that I thought there'd be anything there to do with murder, but it might be interesting to see what his family history looked like. I hadn't asked about how his parents had come to be working for the Mitchells back in the day.

Of course I probably wouldn't be finding out *that* information but I bet myself I could find something interesting.

CHAPTER ELEVEN

As I rode along into the chilly winter wind, with the last of the sun glaring in my eyes, I changed my mind about going home. I'd ride on over to the It'll Grow Back and see if Dixie had a minute. This late in the day she might be done with appointments.

And I sure could use some of her good advice. I didn't like the feeling I was getting being around Vlad. And I figured she'd tell me it was some left over crush from our teenage years before Vlad left for parts unknown. That it'd never gotten to run it's course because of that and now all those old feelings were rising to the top. I'm a grown woman for crying out loud. Not a starry eyed barely teenager.

Plus, good gravy! The man could be guilty of murder. My poor old heart didn't want to believe it, but my stubborn side was sittin' there on my shoulder like that old Devil pointing out that I don't know a dang thing about the grown up Vlad.

And people change from when they're kids. For a whole world of reasons havin' nothing to do with little old me.

I told that Devil voice to just hush it as I cruised up to the beauty shop. Peering through the front window, I saw Dixie by herself sweeping the floor. *Good.* The bell jingled as I pushed through the door, and Dixie looked up in surprise.

"Well hey, Lily Gayle. You've got a look on your face like you need to get something off your chest." She put the broom she was holding into a closet and motioned me to have a seat in the waiting area. Twirling the wand attached to the blinds on the front window she closed the rest of the world out, leaving us sitting cozy and alone in the shop.

"You want something to drink?" she asked. "Not much to be had here this time of day though." She laughed. "I've got some coffee that's only three hours old. We had a bit of a rush this afternoon and nobody drank any of the last pot I made."

"No, thanks." I wrinkled my nose, thinking about all the cups of high dollar, and highly caffeinated, coffee I'd already had today. "I think I've had enough coffee to power a mill generator. I may not sleep for a week."

Eyes wide, she sat next to me on the little couch. "Reeeeally." She leaned back, crossed her legs and gave me her full attention. "Do tell."

So. I got down to brass tacks telling her everything I'd found out about what Vlad'd been up to in the years since we'd seen him last. And the sleep study.

Dixie let me rabbit on without interrupting. She knows me well. When I get on a roll with something it's best to just let me go on full steam ahead and get it all out of my system.

I finally wound down. She waited a long minute before saying anything. I reckon to make sure that was it. Nothing else.

"Well, that's plum amazing. Imagine something like that taking place right here in

Mercy!" She wiggled off the couch. "Come on. Let's get out of here and go to my place where we can get comfortable and finish this little chat." Giving me the hairy eyeball, she went on. "And don't think I don't know there's something you're holding back."

Giving her my best innocent look, I stood up. "I have no idea what you're talkin' about."

She unlocked the door and motioned me out. "You sure do know what I'm talkin' about."

I went through the door and over to my bike.

"Leave it." Dixie said. "Hop in the car with me and we'll head over to my house."

I hesitated, falling behind her fast moving form as she hot-footed over to her car. She turned, saw me still standing on the sidewalk, and frowned. "What?"

I meandered toward the car. "Let's go to my place. I bet Jack's at home and he won't want to hear all the hen talk."

Dixie narrowed her eyes. "If we go to your house you have to promise to tell me what ever it is you're holdin' back right now."

I sighed. "Fine. I'll tell you."

She pumped a fist, hooting in triumph. "I knew there was more. Get on over here in the car. We're wastin' valuable time."

I laughed as I got in. She could always make me do that.

I heard Elliott meowing as I punched in the code to my front door a few minutes later. He wound himself between our legs as we shuffled into the house. Poor kitty. He wanted some attention. I nearly tripped over him twice as I made my way to the fireplace and lit the already laid logs and kindling. I turned and smiled at Dixie. "Have a seat. I'm going to get us some tea."

"I see you still don't have any Christmas decorations up." She hollered behind me as I went down the hall to the kitchen.

I poured two glasses of sweet tea and put some cheese straws on a plate. When I got back to the front room, I found Dixie settled on the loveseat across from the fireplace, shoes off, feet up on the ottoman. Elliott had curled up in his cat bed next to the fireplace and lay snoozing.

I toed off my own shoes and joined Dixie, putting the plate of cheese straws carefully between us.

We drank tea and munched cheese straws in companionable silence, watching the pictures in the flames. Warming up from the chill of the drive over in a cold car. Eventually, her foot nudged mine.

"So. Tell me."

I didn't need to ask what she meant. But I couldn't summon the words, so Dixie helped me out the way only someone who knows you well can do.

"You think Vlad's hotter than a two dollar pistol and that scares you."

I rolled my eyes. "Will you be serious?"

"I am." She said, turning to face me, tucking herself comfortably into the corner of the loveseat. "I know you Lily Gayle Lambert. Better than anybody, I reckon. Except maybe Ben." She tilted her head to the side, considering. "Nope. Not even Ben knows you like I do. I can read you like a book and you had some thoughts, and maybe feelings, while you were up at the old mansion house that you don't want to have."

I stayed quiet. So she went on in a gentle voice.

"John's been gone a long time. It's past time you found somebody to care about, who cares about you." She reached over and took my hand. "You deserve that."

I shrugged. Still not looking at her. "Okay. I think he's good looking." I glared at her. "*Not* 'hot as a two dollar pistol'. What are you, *twelve*?"

She grinned. "Hallelujah!"

I poked her. "Stop it."

She settled back, munching a cheese straw. "So. What's the problem? Is he married? Girlfriend? Just not interested?"

I leaned over the arm of the chair, setting my empty glass on the floor. Buying time. "No. Not married." I said. "And no girlfriend." I paused, pushed my bangs out of my face. "And I think he's interested."

"Well then, what in tarnation seems to be the problem?" Dixies asked, frustration in her voice.

"There *is* the little matter of the murder that happened on his front porch."

That took the wind out of her sails. "You think he's involved?"

"No. Yes. I don't know what to think." I muttered.

"What does Ben say?"

"You know Ben. Everyone's a suspect until he solves the crime."

Dixie was silent for so long, I turned to look at her. Now it was my turn to prod.

"What?"

"Jack's boxing gloves are still missing." Tears welled up in her eyes. "I'm scared, Lily Gayle."

"What? *Why?*"

"What if Jack was involved?"

I thought it over. "What does Jack say? Surely to goodness y'all have discussed it."

She sniffled. "He says he didn't do anything but drive around all night. Swears he has no idea what happened to the boxing gloves."

I watched her carefully. "And you don't believe him?"

"He was calm about the whole thing till I got him all riled up. After I took his head off arguing about how we'd be the laughing stock of the town, Jack was mad enough to spit nails that night. The way only someone who *never* asks for help gets when they finally do break down and ask and get it thrown back in their face the way Tom did to Jack."

CHAPTER TWELVE

The next morning I met up with Dixie in front of Miss Edna's. The big front porch was magnificently decorated for Christmas with silver and gold intertwined garland, miniature trees loaded with ornaments and red ribbons everywhere.

No doubt compliments of Harley Ann's skills. It came near to putting me in a Christmas mood. But even this couldn't quite make it happen.

Dixie and I had managed to solve exactly nothing last night despite talking ourselves hoarse and in numerous circles. We'd consumed two gallons of sweet tea and the whole stock of cheese straws I'd made to last for the entire holiday season.

Dixie stayed scared for and about Jack and I hadn't been able to convince myself that Vlad was completely in the clear. Or that it was okay for me to be having feelings for him. I'd been a widow for nearly ten years and it still seemed wrong somehow. In the end, Dixie had gone home and I'd gone to bed.

Now we were going to visit with Miss Edna while she was enduring her house arrest and see if she could shed any light on old days and old times. When Vlad has lived here as a child and his parent worked up at the mansion.

I didn't think there was much Miss Edna could contribute to the situation s couldn't have known anything about Vlad's childhood, but Dixie insisted she might remember some gossip from back then that might shed some light on things now. I didn't agree, but felt like I should humor her.

Harley Ann met us at the door and ushered us into the front parlor where Miss Edna sat ramrod straight in her chair by the fire on this frosty morning with a full tea cup on the table next to her. She motioned us into the room.

"Bout time you girls came to see me. I was fixin' to defy this ridiculous house arrest order and come find y'all to get the news about the case." She glared at the two of us. "Don't think the two of you are going to cut me out of the action just because I can't investigate with you."

"Now, Miss Edna." I said. "We're not here to fill you in on the case. We're hoping you might remember some old gossip from years ago that might shed some light on things up at the mansion."

Miss Edna's lips went thin. "You are, are you? And you thought I'd be thrilled to fill you in on any details I remember, but you don't plan on including me in figuring out the case?"

Harley Ann put her hand on Miss Edna's arm, but the old woman shook it off.

"I expect that kind of deception from you, Lily Gayle." Her gazed shifted. "But not you, Dixie."

Dixie and I locked eyes.

"How've you been doin', Miss Edna?" Dixie asked, looking back at Miss Edna.

"Now don't you start that polite changin' of the subject with me, Missy." Miss Edna, motioned to Harley Ann to help her get up from the chair. "I heard that your husband is under suspicion in this case."

Dixie's face flamed, and I resisted an itch to snatch Miss Edna baldheaded. I turned, planning to head right on back out the door, but Dixie's hand on my arm stopped me.

"That's right, Miss Edna. He *is* under suspicion. But I don't believe he did anything to Tom Hammond." She gave a tight smile. "And you're under house arrest for doing something you shouldn't have. So I reckon none of us is perfect."

"Don't you sass me, young lady!" Miss Edna snapped, fisting her gnarled hands. Then relaxing them as she took a deep breath. "But you're right to call me out on puttin' you on the spot like that. When I'm in the wrong I say so."

She motioned toward the back of the house. "I apologize for taking out my frustrations on you. I'm fit to be tied over being stuck in the house like this. Normally I don't go out much, but knowing that I can't has made me want to. Don't particularly want somethin' till you can't have it and all that." She made a shooing motion. "Let's all go into the kitchen and sit together while we talk things over."

Even though Miss Edna had a heart of gold under that mean old biddy exterior, I held off on moving. There'd been no call to say that to Dixie and I, for one, wasn't ready to meekly let it go. But it was Dixie's call.

"I hear you're planning to start a food truck business," Dixie said to Harley Ann through the thick air in the room. "I'd be right pleased to try some of your concoctions that Lily Gayle told me about."

We all settled in at the antique kitchen table as Harley Ann poured coffee for everyone. Guess Miss Edna didn't want that tea she'd had sitting on the table next to her after all. Once she'd done that, she pulled the containers of her creations out of the refrigerator, popping them one at a time into the microwave, then bringing them to the table with serving plates and silverware.

The meatballs with peach bourbon glaze were even better than I remembered.

"All of these are amazing, Harley Ann! I bet your food truck will be a great success." Dixie enthused.

"If we find the money to get her started." Grumbled Miss Edna. "Tom Hammond got meaner than a snake with me when I went to him about loaning the money to get her started. I don't know who he thinks he is turning me down like that." She slapped her hand on the table startling all of us. "I'm not a bit surprised he turned up dead. And I'm not a bit sorry that I slipped that castor oil in his punch."

"Now, Aunt Edna," Harley Ann began.

"Don't you try to take up for him, little girl. Somebody must've slipped something a whole heap stronger in his punch than castor oil for him to end up dead the same night. For all we know it could've been Patsy. I know I'd be tempted if I was married to somebody that kept such a tight rein on every little thing I did."

Harley Ann closed her mouth on whatever she'd been about to say. All three of them focused on me.

"Dixie. Do you remember that invisible friend Patsy had when we were kids? I was talking to Ben about it the other night and he didn't remember anything about it."

"Oh my goodness! I'd forgotten all about that." Dixie laughed. "She sure was an odd duck back then"

"What do you mean, back then? She's still weird if you ask me."

"Fine. Fine." Miss Edna interrupted. "But what about some information about the investigation. Spill what you've got."

"I don't know much of anything." I answered.

"I hope you don't think we believe that, Lily Gayle." Responded Miss Edna. "We know you were at the autopsy with Ben, so you must have some information from there."

I sighed. "Not a whole lot, really. There was some kind of bruising in his kidney area that made Doc think Tom'd stumbled against something hard." I was careful not to look at Dixie. But I was wasting my caution.

"Yes. We know Jack's under suspicion about some boxing gloves." Miss Edna said.

"Vlad Templeton's boxing gloves are missing, too." Dixie threw in before I could say anything else.

Miss Edna and Harley Ann looked to me for confirmation. "Yes. That's true." And so much for Ben urging me not to say anything at the autopsy about the boxing gloves. It must be all over town if Miss Edna knew about it -- what with being limited to her house since right after the murder. I figured someone must've called her with the gossip.

"So. Doctor Hottie up the hill may be a murderer." Miss Edna suggested. Trying to get a rise out of me, no doubt.

"It's a possibility." I agreed without addressing the Dr. Hottie portion of the remark.

"Well that sure puts a fly in the ointment." Miss Edna commented.

"I have no idea what you're referring to." I responded, but we all knew I did. Time to get off that subject. "Miss Edna, do you remember any talk about the Mitchells from back in the day?"

"You mean besides all that business about them bein' too high falutin' to associate with us poor town folk?" She gave me a sharp look. "Why are you interested in all that any way? What has it got to do with a murder that took place a few days ago? You tryin' to find some way to excuse Dr. Hottie?"

I flushed. "Of course not. I'm just tryin' to figure out some history here. I remember from when I was doing genealogy research for LizBeth Mitchell that all their help came from somewhere other than Mercy. And, of course, I remember Vlad being home schooled back when we were kids." I glanced at Dixie for confirmation.

And help.

Maybe I *was* trying to cut Vlad some kind of slack by looking for reasons to take him out of the picture for murder. I mean, he'd moved away when he was a kid. So what reason could he have for coming back and murdering the bank manager all these years later?

But something was definitely off up at the Midnight Dragonfly. It'd gotten a vibe off Vlad that felt like he was tiptoeing around something. I just couldn't put my finger on what it could be.

Dixie shrugged. "I don't know what to tell you, Lily Gayle. I haven't seen him yet myself. And I sure never had any doins' with the Mitchells at any time. I don't even remember my parents ever talking about them much. It was kind of like they existed in their own little world up there." She fiddled with her coffee mug. "If we hadn't met Vlad as kids, I'd never have given that family any thought at all."

Harley Ann took Dixie's mug, refilled it and slid it back across the table. Dixie smiled her thanks.

"When I was up there chatting with Vlad, he seemed awfully interested in the genealogy research I did on the Mitchells. Especially the part about the circus connection. I wonder what that was about."

"This isn't gettin' us anywhere." Complained Miss Edna. "What else did you find out at the autopsy?"

"Not much. About the only other really significant piece of information is that the blood work showed a high concentration of Ambien."

"What in Sam hill is that?" Miss Edna wondered.

"It's a prescription sleeping pill."

Dixie's hand jerked and coffee sloshed over the rim of her mug. She jumped up, pulled a wad of paper towels from a roll by the sink and mopped up the spill. All the time avoiding my gaze. I was wondering what in tarnation had spooked her when Miss Edna commented.

"Sleepin' pills." Miss Edna shook her head. "People just need to get up off their behinds and do some physical labor. That'd make 'em sleep just fine."

"I'm thinkin' Dixie and me need to sign up for the sleep study." I blurted out.

Dixie turned astonished eyes to me. "What? Why would we do that?"

"It would be a good way to get information from the inside."

Miss Edna snorted. "What kind of information are you looking for that you need to get involved in some cockamamie study?" She pointed a gnarled finger at me. "Sounds to me like you're looking for an excuse to spend more time with Dr. Hottie."

My temper started heading in the direction of a boil over. Before it could blow, Dixie intervened.

"Besides. Ben would have a fit if we did that."

Miss Edna grunted. "Since when has what Ben wouldn't approve of ever mattered a hill of beans to Lily Gayle?"

CHAPTER THIRTEEN

I was still in a huff when I got back home. I don't know why I let Miss Edna get under my skin. But there you have it. She does it every time.

And Dixie sure hadn't been much help. I reckon she's got herself so tied up in knots worrying about Jack's possible involvement in the murder that she don't know if she's coming, going or already been. And I get that. I know I'd be the same.

After Miss Edna's last insight about me and Ben, and the total lack of support for my idea about signing up to do some inside searching by participating in the sleep study by both of them, I'd been ready to head on out.

I believed Miss Edna's against me and Dixie signing up for the sleep study just because she can't be part of it. Ben hadn't given a time frame for her house arrest. And Dixie. Well, Dixie just had a lot of other things on her mind right now. She'd gone on to the beauty shop for the day and I'd come home to get started on the genealogy research I'd promised myself on the Templeton family.

I lit a fire in the front room, sat in my favorite club chair and fire up my laptop. Elliott came and stretched out across the back of the chair behind my head. His favorite place to be.

I decided to get started on Google since I couldn't remember Vlad's parents' names. If I'd ever even known them. Somebody who'd gotten state funding for a major study must have gotten written up in newspapers or journals before now.

I hit gold on the first search. A dozen articles popped up right off. Clicking on the first one, I settled in to do a little reading before hitting the genealogy sites.

I found the names of his aunt and uncle easily.   Lucy and George Heron. They were mentioned in just about every article. And photographed with him in quite a few with their faces beaming with pride in his accomplishments. As well they should. But finding his parents' names proved to be a lot more elusive. I read fully a dozen articles about him and not once were the names of his parents mentioned.

This little project was going to be considerably more difficult than I'd imagined. I'd envisioned finding their names and popping into the Census records and Bam! Information smorgasbord. I couldn't find them by searching for Vlad because of that pesky seventy-two year rule.

That meant that the most recent census available to me would be the nineteen forty census. Perfect for finding Vlad's parents because I felt sure they'd been born somewhere in the mid-to-late thirties like my own parents.

I couldn't even search for Templeton families in Barkley County in the records because Vlad's family had not been from here. I racked my brain. Trying to pull back any memory, no matter how vague, from childhood that Vlad might have mentioned about his family. Nothing.

I pulled my cell phone out of my pocket and called Dixie. "Do you remember Vlad's parents names?" I asked straight off.

"Who?" Clearly caught off guard, Dixie mumbled to herself. "Oh. Sorry. You caught me in the middle of fixing supper. Hang on a sec." I heard a thumping rumbling sound as she laid the phone down, then heard water running in the background and dishes rattling. She said my name in what must have been a question from Jack about who was on the phone. Another loud rattle, and Dixie was back.

"Okay. I can talk for a minute. Why are you asking me about Vlad's parents?"

"I'm doing some genealogy research on his family and realized I don't know his parents' names. And I can't seem to recall every hearing them. I thought maybe you might."

Dixie sighed. Hummed in a low tone. I waited, know this was her thought process. After a couple of minutes she said. "Nope. I have no memory of ever hearing their names. What about asking Miss Edna?"

"Oh *Lord* no." I protested. "No way am I going to check with her. Besides," I added. "I doubt she'd know anyway. She had even less contact with them than we did."

"We didn't have *any* contact with them." Dixie noted.

"Exactly. So, ergo, Miss Edna had less than zero. Because at least we saw Vlad regularly and might have actually heard him talk about them."

"Yes. But nobody calls their parents by their first name anyway." She observed.

"Hm. That's true. I hadn't thought about it from that angle." I leaned my head back against the chair to think, startling Elliott into jumping down. He gave me a nasty look, then left the room with his tail straight up in outrage. "There's got to be some way to find out." I said to Dixie.

"Well, good luck with it. I've got something fixin' to boil over on the stove. Talk to you later."

I stuck my cell phone back in my pocket, pulled it right back out and opened my Pandora app to listen to some classic rock and roll. As the Stones sang *Satisfaction*, I laid the phone on the table next to me musing that it really sucked that the music of my teenage years was now considered classic.

Back to the issue at hand. Hmm. Hmmm. Where could I locate this information? As *Satisfaction* faded into *Spirit In The Sky*, something stirred in my mind. Death. Vlad's parents had died when we were all kids. Had died *here*. In *Mercy*.

Could there have been an obituary in the local paper? My enthusiasm flagged for a minute. Those at Mitchell Manor hadn't associated with anyone in town, so maybe there wasn't an obituary. But it was definitely worth a try.

Snapping my laptop shut, I shoved it under my chair, grabbed my jacket and headed out to the library. I should have just enough time to run in and check the obituaries for the summer of nineteen seventy-eight before they closed.

Miss Jamerson gave me *the look*, held up her arm and pointed to her watch as I strode through the doors full steam ahead. I held up my hand to forestall any comment. "I know. I know. You're fixin' to close. I promise I'll be quick."

Rushing to the file cabinets that held the micro filmed newspapers, I hoped the project transferring the local newspapers to microfilm that had been going on for almost a year had gotten to the year I needed. The newspaper itself was closed and if what I wanted hadn't made it to microfilm yet I'd be out of luck for this evening.

Glancing over my shoulder, I checked Ms. Jamerson's position. I didn't want her rushing over to offer assistance with my project. She sat at the information desk, looking at something out of my view below the counter. Good.

Scanning the labels slotted into the file cabinet drawers, I sent up a small prayer for divine intervention. And there, on the front of the bottom drawer of the cabinet containing the microfilmed newspapers, the label read 1978. *Yes!*

Pulling open the drawer, I let my fingers follow my eyes as I scanned for the box I wanted. Pulling it from it's slot, I took it to the machine where, with trembling fingers, I loaded the film. Taking a calming breath, I sat down and began scrolling.

Since the Argus is a weekly, all fifty-two papers were on this film. I couldn't remember the exact month Vlad had left town, but it had been toward the end of summer, so I scrolled to July and started scanning obituaries.

Not July. Not August. Could I be wrong about the year? Or, worse, was it not here? Stopping my frantic scrolling, I forced myself to calm down and think clearly. I truly believed it had been late summer and nineteen seventy-eight.

I slowed down, scanning each page of each week's newspaper. And, there, in the August first issue, front page no less, was an article about a multi-car pileup on Interstate -55. Included in the article was the name of the Mercy, Mississippi couple who had lost their lives. Richard and Sara Templeton. *Eureka.*

The overhead lights flicked off, then back on. Startled, I looked around. Ms. Jamerson stood by the door with her hand on the switch, a stern look on her face. Glancing at my Fitbit, I saw that it was already fifteen minutes past closing. So, she'd given me that much grace. A quick glance around the library showed me that no one else was present.

I gave her a quick wave and raised my index finger to let her know I just needed one more minute. I hit the print key and stood so she'd know I was cooperating with the request. Grabbing the sheet of paper with the article off the printer, I folded it and stuck it in my back pocket. Then removed the microfilm from the machine, rolled it properly up and put it back in it's box. Waggling the box in the air, I went over to the file cabinet and returned it to it's proper drawer and slot.

"Thank you for giving me some extra time this evening, Ms. Jamerson." I said as I passed her on my way out. "I really do appreciate it."

She nodded, then cut the lights out. Lucky for me there was enough light coming in the windows from the streetlights that I could get to the front door without falling over something.

Pushing my mean thoughts about Ms. Jamerson to the side, I mounted my bike and raced back home, hardly feeling the cold wind in my face. I had the information I needed to research Vlad's family.

Back home, I settled into my favorite chair again with my laptop and opened my ancestry.com account. Okay. The ages of Richard and Sara Templeton had been listed in the article so I had a pretty good idea for year of birth.

Unfortunately, I didn't have a city or state. And Richard Templeton was not all that unusual of a name. With a little prayer for good luck, I chose the nineteen forty Census records, keyed in the name and the year nineteen thirty-seven.

I clicked on search and, like a little kid, closed my eyes while I waited for the length of time I thought it should take for the results to load. Opening my eyes just tiny bit, I saw a very long page of returns for Richard Templeton.

Shoot. In my rush to find him, I put the year in the wrong box. I entered nineteen thirty-seven as year of birth, and just to be safe, added the plus or minus two years option. Positioning the cursor over the search button, I closed my eyes again and clicked.

Sneaking a squint-eyed peek, I saw there was still a long list of Richard Templetons. *Lord help.* I sighed, put my laptop on the side table and went into the kitchen to pour myself a big ol' glass of sweet tea. I did a few side twists and mini squats to loosen up my back since I was up. Picking up my tea, I went on back to the front room.

Scanning over the list after sipping my tea, I realized I'd done exactly the right thing getting up and walking away. As soon as I scanned the list again, one name jumped out at me. Richard V. Templeton, born circa 1937. *V. Like Vlad.* Could it possibly be? With a shaking finger, I clicked on the entry.

Okay. No full middle name. Just the initial. Well shoot. Parents, William and Matilda. I clicked on the link to take me to information about William. And nearly fell out of my chair. Place of residence: Sarasota, Florida. Occupation: circus performer.

William Templeton had been a circus performer. Family connections to the Mitchells had been circus performers. I'd discovered that when I was doing a genealogy research for LizBeth Mitchell last year.

The circus had been a place for some of the Mitchells with the most severe from of their hereditary hypertrichosis to live a slightly normal life. This *must* be the right connection. And what a connection it was!

But what could it all mean? I hadn't seen Vlad naked or anything, but he didn't seem to have any visible issues with excessive hair growth. The only odd thing about him as a child had been the sugar cubes and shots for diabetes. What had Vlad's grandfather done in the circus? Maybe that was the connection that'd brought Vlad and his parents here all those years ago.

Glancing at the clock I saw it was nearly midnight. Far too late to call Dixie with this information. I'd never get to sleep with all this boiling around in my head, though. Reckon I'd spend some time researching the history of Sarasota, Florida and the circus.

CHAPTER FOURTEEN

By the time the sun came up I was punch drunk from all my research. I believed I had some concrete evidence that Vlad's grandfather had been connected to the circus and something about the connection had led to Vlad's family being employed by the Mitchell's when Vlad was a kid.

I couldn't quite put my finger on why though. Some vital information was not available to me. But I had a feeling my cousin could access it. Being as how he's the sheriff, I figure he can get any information he's got a mind to get. The trick would be persuading him the information was something he wanted to find.

As I coasted my bicycle into the parking lot at the court house, I went over every option I could think of to get Ben to do a search on William V. Templeton. I knew if he figured it was just curiosity on my part he'd never in a million years do the search.

I had a niggling feeling that there was something hiding in the information that would be of value to Ben. Unfortunately, women's intuition wasn't something Ben held with. Only concrete facts.

Taking the stairs down to the basement where the sheriff's office is located, I prayed for divine intervention. I knocked on the door as I opened it. Reenie, Ben's dispatcher, was nowhere to be seen, so I went on back to Ben's office. He must've heard my knock at the door 'cause he was halfway out of his seat when I slipped into the room. Seeing me, he frowned and sat back down.

"What bring you out so early this morning, Lily Gayle?"

"Ben. I've come up with some information about the Templeton family that I think you'll be interested in."

His eyebrows went up to his hairline. "Is that right?"

Sitting down I pulled his visitor chair close enough to his desk that I could lean my elbows on it and give him my most serious stare. "Vlad Templeton's grandfather was a circus performer down in Sarasota, Florida back in the forties."

"And I would be interested in that information because?"

I threw my hands in the air. "Because there's something not right up at the Midnight Dragonfly. Vlad's hiding something."

Shifting in his chair, Ben sighed. "I don't have any reason to think Vlad is involved in the murder or any reason to be interested in some ancient history about his grandfather. There is no way it's related to the murder of Tom Hammond." He paused, giving me the hairy eyeball. "You know I don't use my position to indulge you in your curiosity. And if you rushed over here so early thinking you'd get me to use my position to find information for you on something not related to a criminal act, you wasted your time."

Well, that sure took the wind out of my sails. I knew he'd kick up a fuss. I should've had my argument in better shape before I got here. No sleep in nearly twenty-four hours had my brain running slow. I couldn't for the life of me come up with a reason beyond my own intuition for Ben to conduct the search. Wait though. I *had* seen something odd.

"I saw Vlad Templeton's beat up old truck parked on the town square the night of the Christmas party." I told Ben. "And Vlad's boxing gloves are missing. Did you fingerprint the ones you found up under the bushes at the crime scene?"

Ben frowned, reaching for a folder on the desk. "You know what?" He shuffled pages. "I'm actually glad you came this morning. I need you to go with me to Dixie and Jack's."

Flummoxed by his change in subject matter, I sat back in the chair. "Why are you going there? What's that got to do with Vlad's boxing gloves?"

"I'm going to bring Jack in for questioning about the murder."

"*What!*" I jumped up from my chair. Hands on hips, I glared. "You know good and well that Jack Newsom did *not* murder Tom Hammond."

Ben watched me with sympathetic eyes. "The fingerprints on the boxing gloves are Jack's."

I floundered internally. *Impossible*, screamed my brain. "But....."

"I know." He said. "I'm shocked myself."

As my legs went weak, I maneuvered myself back into the visitor chair. "I will never believe Jack did it." I pushed my fingers through my bangs, thinking. This could not be happening. "Do you have anything other than the fingerprints on the gloves? I mean, that's mighty slim evidence to charge a man with murder."

Ben shuffled more papers. "I agree. I contacted all the pharmacies in the county checking into Ambien prescriptions. Jack has one."

I blew out a breath. "Is he the only person in town with a prescription for it?"

Ben shook his head. "Actually, no. Looks like Vlad picked the perfect town for his sleep study. There's several people in town who have sleep issues. Even Patsy Hammond has a prescription for it. And, of course, Vlad would be able to get it since he's a doctor."

I leaned forward, eager to make Ben see his mistake. "There! If that many people have access to it. Including Vlad, I might add. Then someone other than Jack could have done the murder." Slapping my hand on the desk, I insisted. "There is no way in this world that Jack killed anybody. I don't care if those gloves do have his fingerprints on them. Somebody could have stolen them out of his car."

"Why are you so eager to throw Vlad under the bus on this?" Ben inquired. "What reason would he have to do it?"

Nearly screaming in frustration, I said. "What reason would *Jack* have to do it?"

"He was angry at Tom that night."

"Maybe." I said. "Dixie said he was riled up. But I know Jack wouldn't kill anyone over something so ridiculous as the heat of the moment."

Ben gave me a sad look. "It happens every day, Lily Gayle."

"Not in Mercy." I protested. "And not Jack Newsom."

"And another piece of information." He hesitated, then went on. "Patsy Hammond told me she saw Jack that night. She said he nearly sideswiped her car as she was pulling out of the driveway to the Midnight Dragonfly. So Jack would have a pretty good idea that Tom was up there."

I remembered Patsy saying she'd seen Jack when Ben and I had been out at her house getting the punch bowl and cups. I didn't remember anything about nearly getting sideswiped though. She must've come up with that later.

"Is there nothing else that you found out?" I wondered. "Something that doesn't point to Jack that you're putting aside in your rush to pin it on Jack?"

His eyes went hot, but he answered. "There are a few things that need to be clarified. That's why I'm going to bring Jack in for questioning."

"What things?" I demanded. "Tell me."

Right about then, Ben got his stubborn look. I knew it well. It meant he was fixin' to shut me out. But I wasn't having it.

"You're about to go to my best friend's house and bring her husband in for questioning for murder. You want me to go with you. I assume to keep Dixie from totally losing her mind over it." I paused. "But there are some things that don't quite fit."

He nodded.

"Come on, Ben. Tell me what they are. Two heads. Another person's angle. I don't care how you want me to phrase it. I'll beg on my knees. Just, please tell me."

When he broke eye contact, hope left me. I hadn't convinced him. I put my hands on the arms of the chair, preparing to stand and leave him to his plan. No way would I go with him. I'd ride my bike all five miles out to Dixie's before I'd sit in the car with him on this errand.

My movement must have caught his attention because he motioned me to sit back down. Scared to hope, I eased back down.

Still looking away, he said. "I hope you don't think I enjoy the idea of bringing in one of my closest friends for questioning in a murder."

I kept quiet. Not sure where he was going with this and afraid anything I might say would tip the balance back out of my favor.

He turned back toward me. "There're two things that are odd. But don't get Jack off the hook."

Quiet and still as a mouse. That was me.

"When I talked to some experts involved with the insomnia studies going on in other parts of the country, some of them seemed to think Vlad has some hidden agenda. But they couldn't say why they thought that." He gave me a hard stare. "But, as you already know, I don't deal in feelings. I deal in hard facts."

I couldn't help myself. "So I'm not the only person who thinks there's something off."

He frowned and I shut up. Quick.

"And there's nothing concrete to tie Vlad to the murder."

"But it happened at his home." I pointed out. "And you said it would be easy for a doctor to have access to Ambien."

"And I still don't have a motive for Vlad to have done it. Right now, I need to determine how Jack's boxing gloves got under that bush at the scene of the crime and if he went up to the Midnight Dragonfly after he almost ran over Patsy." He softened his voice. "They're legitimate questions, Lily Gayle. And they have to be asked. Are you going to go with me so you can stay with Dixie?"

CHAPTER FIFTEEN

As we rode east out of town, into the rising sun toward Dixie and Jack's, I tried to mentally prepare myself for their reaction. I felt pretty sure Jack would cooperate. 'Cause he's a law abiding, stand-up guy. Despite Ben taking him in for questioning.

But Dixie might be another matter. It took a lot to make her lose her temper, but once she did, it was in everybody's best interest to stand back and let it run its course or risk getting caught in the fall out. Be it physical or the rough side of her tongue.

I can't decide which one she's likely to lead with today. Mostly because I can't believe I'm sitting here next to Ben on the way to bring in a close friend for questioning in a murder. As I'm pondering the impossibility of the situation, Ben's phone vibrates with a text message.

"See who that is, would you?"

I pick up the phone from the center console and read the message. It's from Vlad. Asking Ben to come up to the Midnight Dragonfly for a talk. I relay the message and Ben frowns.

"It'll have to wait til I'm done with Jack."

"But what if his information clears Jack?" I ask. "Wouldn't you rather find that out before you put Jack and Dixie through this?"

Ben's knuckles go white on the steering wheel, but his voice is calm. "I don't think Vlad has anything to say that's going to clear Jack." He glanced over at me. "I understand how you feel, but we already had this discussion."

I see the kitchen window curtain flick as we pull up in the drive. No doubt Dixie or Jack wondering who's coming to visit this early in the morning. Never dreaming they're about to be blindsided by their closest friends. I wish I'd secretly texted Dixie a heads up. But it's too late now. Jack has the front door open. Big smile on his face. I feel like a total heel.

"Hey, Lily Gayle. Ben. Y'all come on in. Dixie's 'bout got breakfast ready."

I felt lower than a snakes belly as we squeezed past Jack into the house where the scent of sausage cooking greeted us. Dixie peeked around the door from the kitchen, waved a spatula. "Y'all are just in time. Come on in here and have a seat."

Ben and I walked into the kitchen and I hip bumped Dixie away from the stove as I pulled the skillet off the burner.

"What're you *doing*?" Dixie asked as Ben started reading Jack his rights.

I put my hand on her arm but she shook me off. Squaring off in front of Ben, she forced him to look at her. Jack stood behind her, a stunned expression on his face.

"Are you *seriously* reading Jack his rights?" She demanded. "What the *hell*, Ben?"

I reached for her again, but she jerked away from me. "Are *you* in on this?" She asked incredulously.

"Dixie." I said. "Ben says he need to question Jack about some things. He's not being charged with anything at this point."

"What?"

Ben stepped closer. "Now, calm down, Dixie. I need Jack to go with me to the station to answer some questions about the murder. The boxing gloves and his whereabouts that night. On the record."

"Now you just hold on a cotton pickin' minute, Ben Carter. You better have more than that if you think you're takin' my husband off to jail."

"It's alright, Ben. I'll come with you and clear this up. I've got nothing to hide." Jack put his arm around Dixie's shoulders. A move that could have gained him a sharp elbow to the guts, but Dixie slumped like a punctured balloon. All her bravado gone. One whimper escaped her lips. Jack pulled her into a bear hug.

They remained that way while me and Ben looked away in embarrassment. At least, I looked away. I couldn't say what Ben was doing since I wasn't looking in his direction. After a long minute, I heard Jack clear his throat and looked back.

"We'll get this straightened out." He hugged Dixie closer to his side, eyes locked on her. "I promise you I did not do this and it's going to be okay."

Dixie raised her chin and nodded. Stepped back and let Jack walk to Ben. The two of us stood stood watching in silence as the men left the house. As soon as the police cruiser pulled onto the road, Dixie whirled on me.

"I can't believe you are going along with Ben on this."

I raised my hands. "Dixie I tried everything I could to talk him out of it. You know I don't think for a single minute that Jack did anything to Tom."

"Tell me everything you know." She glared at me. "I mean *everything*."

I took a deep breath, getting my thoughts in order before I started talking. "Ben said the boxing gloves he found at the crime scene have Jack's fingerprints."

Dixie shook her head. "I asked Jack about those gloves. He said he's not sure when the last time he paid attention to them was. He kept them in the car so he could go box after work and the gloves would be in the car with his workout clothes." She frowned. "He said he hadn't been to any classes in a couple of weeks because thing were so crazy at work he didn't have time."

"So, how did the gloves get under that bush?"

Dixie gave a choked laugh. "Your guess is as good as mine. You know we never lock the car doors around here. And they weren't locked the night of the Christmas party when it was parked in the town square. Anyone could have seen the gloves and taken them."

"But who did?" I wondered. "Who would want to set Jack up for murder?"

"I can't begin to guess. " Dixie pulled a chair out from the breakfast table and sat heavily. "Jack and I have been over this and over this, but we can't come up with anyone." She turned teary eyes to me.

"I know he did not have anything to do with this. But what if we can't prove it?"

I sat next to her and took her hand. "We're going to make sure we prove he didn't do it."

"What else has Ben got? There must be more than the gloves."

"He said Patsy Hammond told him Jack nearly sideswiped her car as she was coming out of the drive to the Midnight Dragonfly after she dropped Tom off up there. So Ben thinks that means Jack could have known Tom was there."

"That's not right. Jack told me he wasn't anywhere near there that night. Why would Patsy tell Ben that?"

I shook my head. "I don't know. Maybe she was confused? Did Jack say he'd seen her at all when he was out driving around?"

Dixie drummed her fingers on the table, a faraway look on her face. "Nope. I can't remember him saying anything about seeing her." She sat for a few more minutes. "I'm going out there to talk to her. I can't believe she knew what she was saying would get Jack in all this trouble."

"I don't think Ben would like it if we went out there and got Patsy all upset."

"Why are you worried about Ben getting upset?" She stood up, went to the hook where car keys dangled and took them down "I'm going. If you don't want to, then you can wait here."

I stood up. I couldn't let her go by herself.

CHAPTER SIXTEEN

Dixie had already slammed herself into the car by the time I got outside. I hotfooted to the car, yanked open the door and flung myself into the passenger seat as she was cranking the engine.

I'd barely snapped my seatbelt when she floored it out of the driveway and fishtailed onto the county road. As I white knuckled the oh-shit handle, stomach churning, she rocketed down the road toward the Hammonds house. I sent up a silent prayer that we didn't met a car coming the other way because Dixie was taking her half out of the middle.

"Don't you think you should slow down just a bit?" I inquired. "Pulling up in her driveway like a bat out of hell probably isn't the best approach"

For a minute I didn't think she'd heard me, but the the car slowed down a bit and I eased my grip on the oh-shit handle enough to allow blood to flow back into my fingers. "Let's get a plan together before we go busting up in there."

She whipped the car into a side path so fast my head snapped back. I watched as she threw it in park and turned to me.

"I'm so mad right now I can't see straight." She said. "I know Patsy is lying about Jack but I don't understand why she's doing it."

I let go of the handle completely and flexed my fingers.

Dixie pounded her fists on the steering wheel. "Why? Why?"

I reached over and put my hand over hers, holding them still. "I don't know. She's always been a weird duck. Maybe she really thinks she saw Jack."

Dixie uttered a little scream of frustration. Then breathed in and out in deliberate slow motion. "Alright. I've got to calm down. You're right that it won't do a lick of good to go in there making accusations."

"Good idea. Let's just go drop in and see what happens when we ask a few questions."

"Okay." Dixie put the car back in gear, backed onto the county road and proceeded toward Patsy's house a a much more decorous speed that previously.

As we turned into the drive, I noticed that the only car there was the Lexus belonging to the Hammonds.

"Wonder where Lisa is." I commented as Dixie pulled to a stop. "The funeral hasn't taken place yet so she should still be around. Right?"

"I would think so." Dixie said as she opened the door and swung out of the car.

I followed her up to the front door. Everything felt way too quiet. Like the world was maybe holding it's breath. Not a good feeling. I stood behind Dixie as she rang the bell. Since I wasn't Patsy's favorite person, I thought it might be better if she didn't see me till after she'd opened the door.

I heard the door pull open and Patsy said. "Well, hey Dixie. What brings you out here this morning?"

I hoped Dixie would play this right and not make any accusations of lying until after we'd gotten inside and maybe figured out what the heck was going on at this house.

"Hey Patsy. I was out this way and thought I'd stop in and check on you. Especially since I don't see Lisa car here."

Patsy opened the door wider and Dixie stepped in. Patsy looked like she wanted to close the door in my face when she saw me, but motioned me on in after a short hesitation.

I stepped inside to a dim, funky smelling house. What in the world? I heard Patsy turn the deadbolt after she'd closed the door. Dixie turned at the sound and met my eyes. Then looked past me.

"So, Patsy." She said in a casual voice. "How are you holding up? Is there anything we can help you out with?"

Patsy motioned us toward the living room. We sat side by side on the couch facing Patsy.

"I appreciate y'all stopping in to check on me." Patsy picked at the ratty housecoat she'd had on last time I'd seen her. "Lisa went to run some errands. She'll be back in a bit."

Dixie caught my gaze and cut her eyes toward the kitchen. I looked in that direction and knew that's why the house smelled so funky. A bunch of casserole dishes sat uncovered on the kitchen table. Spoiled food. A chill crawled up my spine. Dixie's hand found mine on the cushion between us and gripped hard.

"So, Patsy. We don't want to bother you while you're in mourning." Dixie explained. "But I wanted to talk to you about Jack. You told Ben Carter you'd seen him that night when Tom was killed."

"That's right." Patsy said with a gleam in her eyes. "I did see him. He nearly took the side off my car when I was pulling back out on the highway after I dropped Tom off up at that sleep study."

"Jack said he was never out by the Midnight Dragonfly that night."

"Are you callin' me a liar?" Patsy asked, clenching her fists in her lap.

I squeezed Dixie's hand. Trying to warn her to back off. There was something bad wrong with this woman. Dixie ignored my warning.

"Yes. I am, Patsy. Ben came out to the house this morning to take Jack in for questioning based on your word. But I think you didn't see Jack."

"Well. Obviously Ben believes *me*." Patsy hissed.

Uh. Oh. This had been a very bad idea. I eyed the distance to the front door and remembered the dead bolt was on. Could we get to the door, unlock it and get outside before Patsy went bat shit crazy on us? I didn't much think so.

Apparently Dixie didn't think so either, because she jumped up from the couch, yanked me by the hand and rushed to the bathroom in the hall. She'd caught me off guard, so I stumbled to my knees before catching my balance and following her. She slammed the door shut and turned the pitiful lock on the flimsy, hollow thing.

The door shudder and nearly popped open when something heavy hit it on the other side. Dixie and I both pushed against it, holding it closed.

Out I the hallway, Patsy began ranting.

"Y'all are no better than Tom. Coming out here thinking you're going to catch me out and lock me up."

Something hit the bottom of the door. Her foot?

"He thought he was going to get me sent to the crazy house. But I fooled him." Hysterical laughter started up, giving me the shivers. "Now he won't be sending me anywhere."

"Do you have your phone?" I whispered to Dixie. She shook her head. I pulled my phone from my back pocket, leaned back against the door to keep it braced and tried to call Ben.

It went to voice mail. In a voice barely above a whisper, I left him a message about our situation but wondered how long it might be till he listened to it. We needed help quick. I didn't have much faith in this door holding up for very long if Patsy really decided to break it down.

Right then something slammed hard against it. Her body? Whatever it was bowed the door in toward us. We pushed back hard, managing to hold it closed. For now. But how long?

I tried Jack's phone, but it went to voice mail too.

"Maybe they turned their phones off while Ben is questioning Jack." Suggested Dixie.

Well that was just great. Now what? I called Miss Edna. Who, thank goodness, picked up.

"Hello!"

"Miss Edna." I whispered. "Dixie and I need help"

"Hello?"

Great. She couldn't hear me. And I was leery of talking much louder in case Patsy heard me.

"Lily Gayle! Are you there?" Squawked Miss Edna over the phone. "I saw Ben taking Jack into the courthouse a while ago."

Good gravy. Patsy would hear for sure. I hung up. Pressing the text icon I sent a plea for help.

Me & Dixie at Patsy's. She's the killer. Send help.

Nothing. Then dots. Thank goodness!

This is Harley Ann. I'm going to the courthouse to get the sheriff. Hang on.

I tilted the phone so Dixie could read the message. She nodded. We pressed our backs to the door.

Right then, we heard a gun cock out in the hallway. Not the racking of a shotgun. But still a sound to make your flesh shiver. With only this hollow door between us and the crazy woman out there, even a pistol could kill one or both of us.

"Y'all come on out of there now. Don't make me shoot through this door."

Dixie and I locked eyes. Should we?

"I mean it." Shouted Patsy. "Y'all just couldn't leave well enough alone. Now I'm gonna have to kill you both."

"There's no way I'd let Jack go to prison for something he didn't do." Dixie shouted back.

I jabbed her with my elbow. "Have you lost your mind?"

A bullet blasted through the door just over our heads, went through the shower curtain across from us and broke something on the other side.

As I hit the floor for safety, excitement coursed through me. Was there a window on the other side of that shower curtain? Dixie had dropped right next to me. I belly crawled over to the tub and peeked behind the curtain. Broken window glass littered the tub.

I turned my head and nodded at Dixie. She braced her hands against the tub and her feet against the door to get the best pressure on it as I eased over into the tub avoiding the broken shards. I turned the window lock and pushed gingerly on the window. It slide up without a sound. I punched the screen lose, then grabbed a towel off the rack using it to cover the broken glass lying on the ledge.

Poking my head around the side of the curtain, I motioned Dixie to come on. She eased up off the floor. We both cocked our heads, listening. Silence. The window was small, but fortunately both of us were slim enough to squeeze through.

Dixie motioned me to go first and I shook my head. She leveled her hand above my head. Then above hers. Pointing out that I'm shorter and needed a boost. I sighed and let her boost me up high enough that I could get my upper body out the window.

I pulled myself through listening every second for the sound of another gunshot or the door busting open. It stayed quiet. Dixie pulled herself into the window and I helped her ease through and down to the ground.

Crouching low, we rounded the corner of the house just as Ben pulled into the driveway, Jack beside him. He'd come in with no sirens. Dixie ran toward the car as Jack got out. Just like a Hallmark commercial. I couldn't help but smile.

CHAPTER SEVENTEEN

Two days later, when everything had calmed down. When Patsy Hammond had been taken to a psychiatric hospital for evaluation – and probably to stay on an insanity plea – Ben and I were headed up to the Midnight Dragonfly.

Vlad had called and asked that both of us pay him a visit. I hoped I was going to get answers to my questions about his family.

He met us at the door and ushered us into the kitchen. Once we'd gotten our coffee and sat down at the table, Vlad seemed a bit hesitant to speak.

"What's this all about?" I asked, hoping to get the conversation started.

Vlad fiddled with a placemat on the table, avoiding looking at either of us. The suave, confident doctor had disappeared. This man had discomfort written all over him. Eventually he began.

"Y'all know I'm here on a state funded sleep study program."

We nodded.

"There's a little more to it than I originally said."

I looked at Ben.

"You're not planning on doing anything illegal up here, are you?" Ben questioned.

Vlad remained silent for a minute. Then, "It's not illegal in Mississippi."

"But it *is* illegal in other states?"

Vlad nodded.

"Why don't you tell me what it is you're planning to do."

Vlad shifted in his chair. I could see that he was uncomfortable. Why had he called us to come up here to listen to something he so obviously didn't want to tell us.

"As part of the genetic testing, I'm looking for a particular gene that has been found in people with insomnia."

Ben and I nodded.

"And, I wanted to study several generations in order to track this gene. So that's one reason why I came back to Mercy. It's a small town where several generations of families live."

We nodded again.

"But I'm also looking for another genetic anomaly."

Ben and I exchanged looks.

"Does this have something to do with the hypertrichosis gene in the Mitchell family?" I asked.

Vlad looked uneasy. "Partially."

Ben shifted. "Why don't you just spell it out for us, Vlad?"

"Most of the people, including my parents, who worked for the Mitchells had connections to the old circus circuit."

Eureka! I'd been right about that.

"And a lot of them, again including my parents – and me, too – carry genetic mutations."

What? Genetic mutations? Did Vlad have the hypertrichosis gene after all?

Almost as though reading my mind, Vlad went on. "I don't have the hypertrichosis gene. That was the Mitchells." He paused, took a breath. "I have the porphyria gene."

"So. What's that in plain English?" Ben asked sarcastically.

"It's sometime considered a form of vampirism."

My hand jerked, knocking my coffee over. I scrambled to get a kitchen towel to mop up the mess.

"Remember when we were kids? How we always played in the woods? For me it was because of a reaction to sunlight. It's not as bad for me as for some." He paused.

Neither Ben nor I said anything. What could we say? Our old friend had dropped a major bomb on us. I felt sure Ben was still trying to process what Vlad had intended to do with his genetic sampling.

"And the sugar cubes?" Vlad smiled at me and I remembered asking him about them the last time I'd been up here. Had it only been a few days ago? "The sugar helped me to control symptoms."

Ben and I sat stunned. Then Ben said. "What were you planning to do during your sleep study genetic testing that isn't illegal in Mississippi?"

Vlad flushed dark red. "My plan was to test all the participants for genetic mutations that may be tied to hypertrichosis and/or porphyria."

"So you're assumption is that your ancestors. And the Mitchell ancestors. And pretty much all the circus people who lived here over the last hundred years or so, were having affairs with locals and have transmitted these genetic anomalies to the people in town?" I asked.

I looked at Ben. "I've heard enough. I'm leaving."

CHAPTER EIGHTEEN

"Are you *knitting* now?" Ben asked in a disbelieving tone as we sat in my front room relaxing after the long week we'd just had.

"Mamaw Waddell taught *both* of us, way back in the day."

"Those are some memories I'd just as soon forget. I still can't believe Mama made me go to Mamaw and learn to knit with you."

I laughed remembering the rough-and-tumble little boy struggling with the needles and yarn. "I bet you could whip up a scarf right now if you needed to."

"*That'll* never happen." He frowned at me. "And you just keep those memories to yourself. I don't need all that teasing that'll come from everyone if you remind them."

I sighed. "I haven't knitted for years. I decided it would be a good way to relax on long evenings this winter. I'm just going to do a lap blanket to start. Nothing complicated."

Ben shook his head. "Seems to me like you've got enough going on with the dress business, the genealogy and, now, the thing with the food truck. Who the heck needs food truck in Mercy? But, far be it from me to tell you what to do."

I arched one eyebrow. "Really. You seem to do it all the time so I don't know what you mean. Besides. It's Harley Ann with the food truck not me. I'm just trying to help her get going."

Ben sighed and stretched his legs in front of him, getting his feet closer to the fire. The big toe on his right foot stuck out through a hole in his sock. Mentally I shook my head. For such a good sheriff, he sure didn't take care of himself as well as he took care of the citizens of Mercy.

After a few minutes of silence, he said, "So basically, Patsy killed Tom and set it up so that either Jack or Vlad would the fall for it." Shaking his head he added, "And almost got away with it."

"Well thank goodness she didn't."

We sat quietly for a bit. Comfortable with each other's company.

"You like him." Ben said.

Startled from my contemplation of the flames in the fireplace, I asked. "Who?"

"You know who."

I frowned. "He lied to me, Ben. I don't know what to make of that."

"He didn't lie." Ben paused. "He just didn't tell us everything. That's different. I've gotten over the shock. And I think I understand why he wants to conduct the study."

"What kind of bullshit man logic is that?" I countered in annoyance. "He showed up here, with a pocket full of covert intentions, planning to take advantage of all of us."

Ben scratched his five o'clock shadow. "I suppose you're right about his original intentions.

But you have to give him credit for coming clean. At least to you and me."

He stood and stretched, making his spine crack. Lowering his arms, he said, "Well. I'm headed home. Lock up tight behind me."

After his tail lights disappeared into the night, I dead-bolted the door, cut the porch light off and went back to my comfy chair by the now dying fire. My knitting needles clicked quietly along a row as I thought over everything that had happened since the Mistletoe Magic Extravaganza.

Vlad showing up to run a sleep study that turned out to be a cover for his own personal agenda. Ben was right. I *did* like Vlad. A lot. But there was a lot of issues to deal with before I would be willing to admit that to anybody but myself. And Dixie.

Miss Edna seemed pretty subdued these days. But I didn't think that would last long. Given her nature, I would bet money she'd be back to her old self by next week. Especially since she now had her great niece's business launch to help plan. I couldn't wait to try some more of those delicious foods as soon as Harley Ann got set up with her food.

As I banked the last of the fire, Elliott came out from behind the wood box and meowed at me. I picked him up and the two of us went upstairs to get some well-deserved shut eye.

RECIPES

Jeannie D's Banana Strawberry Bread

(with permission from Jeannie Daniel)

1 teaspoon vanilla extract

1 cup sugar

1/2 cup margarine

2 eggs

2 overly ripe bananas

11/4 cups all purpose flour

1/2 teaspoon salt

1/4 teaspoon cinnamon

1 teaspoon baking soda

2 tablespoons strawberry jam (I use Aunt Pearlies (which is my daughters company) but you could use any good brand

Bake   at   350   for   hour Cream sugar and butter together. Add eggs and bananas, mix well. Add cinnamon, strawberry jam and vanilla. Mix well, add flour, salt, baking soda. Pour into greased, floured 9x5 loaf pan. Cool 15 to 20 minutes in pan then remove and cool completely.

Hummingbird Cake

3 ½ cups all purpose flour

2 cups sugar

3 eggs

1 teaspoon salt

1 teaspoon baking soda

2 teaspoons vanilla extract

1 teaspoon cinnamon

2 cups vegetable oil

1 ½ cups crushed pineapple, drained

1 ½ cups pecan pieces

3 bananas cut into ¼ inch slices

Preheat oven to 350 degrees

Combine dry ingredients

Beat eggs, combine with oil, stir in vanilla and add to dry ingredients

Fold in bananas, crushed pineapple and pecan pieces

Pour into greased 9 x 13 cake pan

Bake till golden brown and toothpick test is clean

Approximately 45 minutes

Frosting:

1 stick butter, room temperature

8 oz. cream cheese, room temperature

3 ½ cups confectioner sugar

2 teaspoons vanilla extract

Place all ingredients in blender and combine.

Frost cake when cool

If layered style cake is desired, divide cake mixture into two round pans and back until golden and toothpick test is clean. Frost between layers and on top

Sprinkle top with pecan pieces

Jammin' Vegan Chocolate Cupcakes with Peppermint Cream Frosting

(Thanks, Kelly Braun)

2 cups all purpose flour

1 teaspoon baking soda

1 ¼ cup pure cane sugar

½ cup unsweetened cocoa powder

1 cup almond milk

Pinch salt

½ cup coconut oil

1 teaspoon apple cider vinegar

1 teaspoon pure vanilla extract

Preheat oven to 350 degrees

Mix dry ingredients in a medium bowl

Mix wet ingredients in separate medium bowl

Fold mixes together

Pour mix into muffin pan with cupcake liners and bake for 16 to 18 minutes

Frosting:

2 oz. white chocolate chips, melted
4 oz. cream cheese, room temperature
¼ stick unsalted butter, room temperature
1 teaspoon peppermint extract
4 cups confectioner sugar
Peppermint candy, crushed (for topping)

Combine butter and cream cheese in food processor. Slowly add melted chocolate until blended. Add peppermint extract. Slowly blend in confectioner sugar until desired consistency is reached.

Frost cooled cupcakes and sprinkle crushed peppermint candy on top.

Jammin' Meatball Sub with Peach Bourbon Glaze

(Thanks, LuAnn Summers)

Meatballs

1 lb. ground beef

½ cup onion, chopped fine

1 egg

½ cup bread crumbs

2 cloves garlic, minced

4 Tablespoons catsup

Pinch salt and pepper

½ cup grated Parmesan cheese

1 Tablespoon Italian seasoning

Preheat oven to 350 degrees

Mix all together and form into golf ball size balls. Place on parchment paper lined baking sheet. Bake 30 minutes, until meatballs are browned.

Peach Bourbon Glaze

1 peach, peeled and diced small
1 10 oz. jar pepper jelly made with jalapenos
1 tablespoons bourbon

Place all ingredients in small pan and cook on low until combined and syrupy.

Place meatballs on sub roll and drizzle with peach bourbon glaze. Serve hot.

52423414R00130

Made in the USA
Middletown, DE
18 November 2017